# ANGEL AT TROUBLESOME CREEK

## THE BEELER LARGE PRINT MYSTERY SERIES

Edited by Audrey A. Lesko

# ANGEL AT TROUBLESOME CREEK

## Mignon F. Ballard

BEELER LARGE PRINT
Hampton Falls, New Hampshire, 2000

Library of Congress Cataloging-in-Publication Data
Ballard, Mignon Franklin.
  Angel at Troublesome Creek / Mignon F. Ballard
  p.      cm.—(The Beeler Large Print mystery series)
  ISBN 1-57490-275-X (acid-free paper)
  1. Large type books. I. Title

PS3552.A466 A84 2000
  813'.54—dc21                                    00-026117

Published in Large Print by arrangement with
St. Martin's Press, 175 Fifth Avenue, New York, N.Y. 10010
Jacket design by Shea M. Kornblum
Jack illustration by Ed Parker


BEELER LARGE PRINT
is published by
Thomas T. Beeler, *Publisher*
Post Office Box 659
Hampton Falls, New Hampshire 03844


Typeset in 16 point Times New Roman type.
Printed on acid-free paper, sewn and bound by
Sheridan Books in Chelsea, Michigan.

**For Sayre**
**our own angel, with love**

With special thanks to my agent, Laura Langlie, and to my "sister in crime," Tamar Myers, and fellow members of our Charlotte Writers' Workshop.

I would also like to acknowledge St. Martin's' Hope Dellon and Regan Graves for their editorial guidance.

# ANGEL AT TROUBLESOME CREEK

# CHAPTER 1

I, MARY GEORGE MURPHY, WAS AT THE END OF MY rope. And then it broke.

Okay, so I chickened out and latched on to the banisters before that rotten old cord gave way, but you'd think I could do at least one thing right in my life. Now, it seemed, I couldn't even put a merciful end to it. The night before I hadn't enough gas in the car to properly asphyxiate myself in the closed garage, and those sleeping pills dissolved in hot tea tasted so bad I couldn't get it down. Like liquid garlic. Awful! Makes me gag to think of it.

Now maybe whoever killed Aunt Caroline will finish the job for me. I only hope they'll do it as quickly and as painlessly as possible.

The police might think my aunt's death was an accident, but I know better. Aunt Caroline wouldn't have been messing around at the top of those attic stairs unless somebody was with her. And whoever it was must have given her a push. But why?

I crawled to my knees in Aunt Caroline's dusty back hall where my only kin had died four days before and slapped at the grime on my pants. "Damn!" I hollered as loud as I could. "Damn! Damn! Damn!" Why couldn't I at least have sense enough not to try to kill myself wearing white?

Disgusted, I pulled the frayed noose from my neck, sat on the bottom step where they'd found my aunt's twisted body, and cried.

"I've heard just about enough of that," someone said behind me. "And do you really think it's necessary to

1

use profanity? It makes you sound so coarse."

She sat on the stairs above me looking as if she'd just stepped out of an old movie and stopped to rest a minute. She wore a fitted suit—Easter grass green— with a skirt that came just to her knees. Her almost-hat, a little bit of fluff with a little bit of veil, sat atop braided hair the color of nutmeg. "Will you look at that?" the strange woman said with a frown. "I've a snag in my rayons. Now I'll have to stand in line who knows how long to get another pair!"

"*What*? Who are you? Are you nuts or something? What on earth are you doing here?" I stood and backed away from her. If this crazy woman on Aunt Caroline's attic stairs decided to rush me, I wanted as much room between us as possible.

"Earth. Oh, good, then I *am* in the right place." When she stood, I could see she wasn't quite as tall as I was, and I'm a fraction under five eight, and was just a shade on the plus side of chubby. "Been a while, you know," she said, bending to straighten her seam.

"No, I don't know, and if you don't explain yourself in about three seconds, I'm calling the police." For the first time I noticed the woman's thick-heeled shoes. Ugly. Mega-ugly. Looked uncomfortable too.

But what did that matter if the stranger ran me through with the menacing hat pin she wore? I was going to die anyway, wasn't I? If only I could figure out a way to do it. Sniffing again, I searched my pockets for a tissue.

"Here, now, don't be such a sad sack." The arrogant woman stepped down and pressed into my hands a dainty, lace-edged hankie that smelled faintly of strawberries. Then, glimpsing her reflection in Aunt Caroline's streaky hall mirror, she paused to adjust her

2

ridiculous hat.

"Apparently I've been assigned to you," she said. "Although I'm beginning to wonder if I'm not in over my head. If you've snafued the rest of your life like you have the last twenty-four hours, seems I'll have my work cut out for me."

"Excuse me. Just what do you mean by that?" The gauge on my temper valve whirled past Hyperventilate and came dangerously close to what Aunt Caroline would call a Bad-Word Situation, just as it had the week before when my office manager at MultiPack Industries asked me to pick up (one) his cleaning, (two) his coffee, and (three) his bratty kids from nursery school. Unfortunately I had dispensed several of my choice selections on the spot.

The strange lady in green took a lipstick from her purse and applied it carefully, then observed herself for a minute, obviously liking what she saw. "New color— 'Fighting Red'—don't you love it?" She tossed the lipstick into her bag and sat on the big oak chest in the hallway, the one where Aunt Caroline kept extra blankets, and patted the space beside her. "Here, for heaven's sake, I won't hurt you, although I don't know why you're worried if you really mean to do away with yourself."

"Well, of course I really mean to—eventually!" I touched the raw rope burn on my neck. "Do you imagine I *like* thinking up ways to kill myself?"

The woman smiled at me and shook her head until the saucy veil ruffled her elegant eyebrows.

"Why won't you believe me?" I said. And why should I care if this intruder in the Greer Garson suit believed me or not? But strangely I did care.

I watched her walk over and pick up the discarded

3

rope, wondering how she could move gracefully in such shoes.

"Just look at this." She dangled the rope in front of me. "Rotten. Frayed. Where did you get it?"

I shrugged. "Found it—hanging in the garage."

"I see. And how long do you imagine it's been there? Don't tell me you didn't suppose—even hope—that old piece of rope might give way before you grabbed a convenient stair railing."

How did she know? I jumped to my feet, shoving her aside so that the silly hat slid over one small, perfect ear. "Now listen—"

"No, you listen, Mary George Murphy." I felt myself being pressed firmly back onto the seat. How could someone this prim-looking be so strong? "Let's talk about last night in the garage," the woman said.

"How do you know about that? And who told you my name?"

"Never mind. Don't you think if you really wanted to kill yourself, you'd have remembered to buy gasoline? And need I remind you just how thoughtless and wasteful that was with rationing the way it is?"

"Rationing?" Was she serious, or did she just have a warped sense of humor? I was beginning to get a peculiar sensation in my head. Scary.

"And the tea," the woman went on. "Nasty as it was, if you were serious about taking those pills, you'd have held your nose and forced them down. After all, what's a little garlic?"

So it *was* garlic! "But—how—are you clairvoyant or something?"

She leaned against the newel post, crossed her rayon-clad ankles and smiled.

"Don't tell me you've forgotten your aunt's habit of

4

switching things from one container to another. When she used up the garlic in that jar, your aunt Caroline stored her extra teabags there, then forgot about them. They've been on that shelf since last fall."

*This is impossible*, I thought. *How could anyone know these things?* Yet it sounded just like something my aunt would do. I closed my eyes—just for a second; the woman was still there. Maybe I *had* succeeded in killing myself. I was in some sort of limbo zone, or hallucinating from lack of oxygen. I patted the wall behind me. It seemed solid enough—familiar flower basket design, once a bold burgundy, now a listless pink—like the last rose of summer, Aunt Caroline joked. And the paper peeled in that same spot above my head. Beside me my aunt's blue-striped umbrella leaned in the tarnished brass stand. I felt my pulse. A little rapid, but strong. "I don't understand," I said.

"Don't worry, you're not dead."

"You sound disappointed," I said. "Am I supposed to be?"

"Certainly not. If that were the case, I wouldn't be here." The woman cocked her bright head and sniffed. "Is that really chocolate I smell?"

I nodded. "Fudge cake. Delia Sims from across the street brought it over this morning. She and Aunt Caroline were close friends—best friends, really—and—hey, could we backtrack here for a minute? Exactly why *are* you here? I don't believe you told me your name."

"My oversight. Please excuse." The woman pulled off her hat to smooth her glorious hair, and for a moment I thought I saw a flicker of a glow. The radiance of it made me blink. The visitor held out a slender hand. "Augusta. Augusta Goodnight. I'm your guardian angel.

5

"Now, do you think I could have a piece of that cake?"

An angel. Well, why not? I looked at a spot on the ceiling to avoid her eyes. *Just humor her, Mary George. Surely someone will come for her soon.* I didn't believe the woman was dangerous.

"Of course," I said. "I didn't know angels were into food."

"It isn't absolutely necessary, but I haven't had chocolate since . . . well, since I was here last. And with the shortage and all . . ." Her voice dropped to a whisper. "Where did your neighbor get all that sugar? It's not black market, is it?"

"Oh, I'm sure it isn't." I led the way into the kitchen, making sure there weren't any sharp knives lying about. Aunt Caroline's big old house seemed bleak and empty without her. The rest of the world looked much the same.

I puttered about the kitchen, watered the African violets drooping in the window while keeping an eye on my cake-eating guest. Aunt Caroline's favorite cookbook, *Troublesome Creek Cooks,* published by the local Women's Club, lay open to the dessert section, its pages splotched with food and use. My aunt had been president of the club for years, and her recipe for blackberry cobbler was in there, as well as favorite dishes of many of her friends—familiar foods I'd grown up with. She was due to entertain her bridge club this week and had circled that sinfully fattening coffee-based concoction made with dates, nuts, and real whipping cream. Her silly apron with the pigs on it hung by the sink. I gulped back a sob.

Augusta Goodnight finished her fudge cake and dabbed her mouth with a paper napkin, which she

6

folded and put into her large handbag. "Now," she said, "why don't you tell me why you think you want to end it all? Is it because of your aunt, or something else? A Dear John from your sweetheart? A flyboy, I'll bet. You'd think they were the only ones with wings."

I put on a pot of coffee. Yes, real coffee, I assured my guest, and sat down to wait for it to brew. So what if this person had escaped from a lunatic asylum? At least she seemed interested, and now that Aunt Caroline was gone, she was the only one who was.

Before I knew it, I found myself telling her about being dumped two months before the wedding by my fiancé, Todd Burkholder, pond scum extraordinaire. Three weeks after that hussy aerobics instructor moved in next door to him, his mind turned into tofu.

Augusta tasted her coffee and made happy noises. "Well, you're no Betty Grable, but you have potential. Besides, obviously he wasn't the one for you. Sounds like a glamour boy to me. Not worth the worry, dear."

True, but still degrading. And I hurt. Bad. I could scarcely bear to speak his name. And then there had been that unpleasantness at work, I said. Consequently I was fired.

Augusta held up her cup for more. "And what work was that? Tell me about it."

"Not much to tell. Filing mostly, but I had a chance to move up."

"Move up to what?" Augusta yawned.

"Well, assistant manager. Manager. I only went to college a couple of years. Jobs are hard to find." Aunt Caroline did the best she could for me after Uncle Henry died, and I always meant to go back to school, maybe become a teacher, work with young children. Kindergarten age. I remembered what it was like to be

7

five. And alone.

"If you're really my guardian angel," I said, "where were you when my parents were killed in that wreck, leaving me to fend for myself with a name like Mary *George*?"

"I'm getting to that." Augusta took another sip and looked at her watch. "But first, what time does *Charlie McCarthy* come on? I've really missed that show."

"Who? Come on where?"

"Why, the radio, of course! Surely you listen to *Edgar Bergen and Charlie McCarthy*! I know Charlie's just a dummy, but he seems real to me. And Edgar's so patient with him. They always make me laugh."

I tried to explain about Charlie McCarthy and radio in general, but I don't think she believed me. I didn't want to even attempt to bring her up to date on the subject of television.

"Seems to me if you were my guardian angel all this time, you'd know what was or wasn't on the radio," I said. "And what's all this about rationing? We don't have—"

Augusta put down her cup. "Did I say I was always your guardian angel? I don't think so. I believe you misunderstood."

"Oh. Then you weren't responsible for my landing in a pile of leaves when Daddy's car slammed into that big tree?" I had been five when my parents died, but I'll never forget that horrible day. Since I had no living relatives, I was taken to the children's home at Summerwood Acres where I cried every day for a week. Until Sam befriended me. Sam. A funny little boy with hair that wouldn't stay down and a turtle named Imogene. Together we waded in the creek and wandered through fields where daisies grew, eating blackberries

8

until our lips turned purple. I almost smiled. I hadn't thought of Sam in ages until Aunt Caroline sent me that old clipping.

Only a few weeks before I had received in the mail a yellowed, dog-eared newspaper photograph of a long ago Easter-egg hunt at Summerwood. It showed Sam, who must've been about ten, and me sitting on the lawn in front of the main building sharing a chocolate egg. It was the prize egg, which Sam had found, and since I didn't find many that day, he had generously but oh-so-slowly peeled off the golden foil and divided his gooey treasure with me. A reporter snapped the picture and it made the Charlotte paper.

While dusting the living-room bookshelves, my aunt had discovered it in the pages of a book of poems where she'd placed it years before. She mailed it to me with a short but loving note.

> *When we saw this picture, your uncle Henry and I knew you were the little girl we'd been waiting for. A month later you were right here with us in Troublesome Creek—where we knew you belonged! Ran across this recently while cleaning and thought you'd like to have it.*
>
> *With much love your*
> *aunt Caroline*

I thought of Sam now as I had many times since Aunt Caroline sent me the clipping. Where was he now? And would he remember me? I glanced at Augusta Goodnight, whose lips were moving, but I hadn't heard a word she'd said. "What?" I said.

"Hortense. I said your guardian angel was Hortense." The woman studied her neat, pink nails. "Say, you

9

wouldn't have an emery board, would you?

"Oh, never mind," she added, apparently noticing my chewed nubs.

"*Hortense*? My guardian angel's named Hortense?" I tried not to laugh. Didn't want to offend her, maybe send her over the edge.

"That's right. But she's on R and R just now. I'm merely filling in."

So I had a stand-in angel. With my luck, I could almost believe it.

"I'm usually in charge of strawberries," she said. "Or at least five hundred acres of them. It's a big place up there."

"They have five hundred acres of strawberries in heaven? Why?"

"Oh, more than that! Much more than that. Think of all the people who say, 'I don't want to go to heaven if there are no strawberries.' Same thing goes for animals. One of my best friends works on a puppy farm, another spends most of her time not calling cats. Cats hate to be called. Being ignored is pure heaven to them." Augusta Goodnight looked gloomily into the empty coffeepot and turned away. "Of course I also dabble in flowers. We've so many of them there. I didn't want to mention it, but I'm afraid you've overwatered those violets."

I leaned over the table to face her. "Okay, since you seem to know so much, how did my aunt end up at the bottom of those attic stairs? Who *did* kill Aunt Caroline?"

"Oh, I can't tell you that," she said.

"What do you mean, you can't tell me? Why not?"

Her eyes were wide and innocent. "Because I don't know. I'm an angel, dear, not a clairvoyant. Besides . . ." Augusta Goodnight air-touched my face. "I imagine that's for you to find out."

10

# CHAPTER 2

D O I LOOK LIKE NANCY DREW?" I SAID. "MAYBE you'd better go back to gardening." I wasn't doing such a great job of *living*. What made her think I could handle the puzzle of Aunt Caroline's death?

"Don't give up on me yet, I'll get the hang of it again," Augusta said with a smile that was truly radiant. "After all, I did all right for Lucille Pettigrew."

"Who's that?"

"Lucille Pettigrew—my last assignment—lived to be eighty-seven. Wanted to see her grandson home from France, and she did. What a grand day that was! I hadn't been as thrilled since Luther Burbank himself complimented me on my Shasta daisies." Augusta studied me with a slight frown. "Corporal Gordon Pettigrew. Wonder if he ever married that girl he was writing to. He'd be about your age—good-looking too. Took a shell at Normandy. Didn't lose the leg, but I'm afraid he'll always walk with a slight limp."

"Are you talking about Normandy as in *France?* Just how old do you think I am?" I glanced at my reflection in the toaster and wiped a smudge from my cheek. I knew I wasn't looking my best, but still—

"I know exactly how old you are, you're twenty-six. They fill us in on background information before we come. That's how I knew about your aunt's storing tea bags in the garlic jar."

Poor Aunt Caroline. The coroner said it looked as though she'd fallen from the top of the attic stairs. But what in the world was she doing up there? She always got out of breath climbing those steep steps, and I had made her promise she wouldn't go up there alone. I

11

didn't think my aunt would go back on her word. The delicate hankie Augusta had given me earlier was in a damp wad in my pants pocket, but I used it anyway.

When I looked up, Augusta was beside me. She smelled of fresh strawberries and mint, and the touch of her small hand made me feel lighter somehow. "I know how terrible you must feel about your aunt," she said. "But you will heal, I promise. It just takes time."

"She wasn't really my aunt," I explained, "but she was all I had, and I loved her. She and Uncle Henry took me in when I was barely eight; except for my parents, they were the only people who ever really cared about me . . . unless you count this one little boy back at Summerwood Acres." Sam. I remembered how he'd comforted me when I first came to Summerwood and was so afraid of the dark. "Night is just day painted over, Mary G.," Sam reasoned. And I've never forgotten it. "He probably wouldn't remember me now," I said.

Augusta consulted a small notebook she'd taken from her seemingly bottomless handbag, and apparently finding nothing there, put it back with a click of the catch. "We don't know that," she said, "so we'll just have to find out, won't we? But first, I think you should decide what you're going to do."

"Do?" I hadn't thought further than jumping off the kitchen stool in the back hall with a rope around my neck. And I don't care what Augusta Goodnight says, that rope seemed sturdy enough at the time!

"With your life. You have to have someplace to live, work—unless, of course, you're independently wealthy. Did I overlook that in my notes?"

I would've laughed had I been so inclined. Not only was I not wealthy, Aunt Caroline had left several outstanding debts. Large debts. Already creditors were breathing down my neck, and there was barely enough to pay funeral expenses. "I guess the first thing to do is try and sell this place," I said. The big old house on Snapfinger Road was drafty and in need of repairs, but it was the only real home I'd known since Daddy took a notion to pass on a hill and made an orphan of me. I frowned. "And I guess the furniture must be worth something. Delia would know."

"Delia? The black-market sugar neighbor who made that heavenly fudge cake?"

"She used to have an antique shop," I said. "And why do you keep carrying on about sugar? Sugar isn't rationed. Obviously you didn't get the message up there in your strawberry patch—or wherever—but World War Two has been over for fifty years."

Augusta sat so hard her little hat slid clear to the middle of her nose. "Now you're joshing me," she said.

"I'm not in a joshing mood."

"Fifty years! My goodness . . . We did win, didn't we? Tell me we won."

I nodded. "At a price." I thought of the losses on D day, and there was a monument here in the park to all the local servicemen who died in that war. Too many. And of course I'd read about Hiroshima and Nagasaki.

"We have no way to measure time in heaven," Augusta said. "No watches, no calendars—not even a sundial. Don't need them." She smiled. "Does this mean you can have all the sugar you want? And cheese and coffee? And gasoline—what about gasoline?"

"That too." I watched the woman's face for any sign she was faking. She was either a very good actress or a genuine loony.

"In that case," Augusta said, "could I please have another piece of that cake?"

13

"Be my guest. In fact, I'll have one with you." I hated to acknowledge it, but I was getting hungry. It was the first sign of an appetite since my whole life began to plunge into the basement.

I uncovered the cake and looked at it closely. I could've sworn I'd served a larger portion than what appeared to be missing, but the chocolate cake looked as if it had hardly been touched.

Augusta swung her foot as she watched me cut two generous wedges and fill glasses with milk. "Do you think we might drop by the shoe store this afternoon? I'd really like to get rid of these clodhoppers."

I made a face at the woman's hideous footwear. "Good idea. But just how long *do* you plan to stay?"

"Here's lookin' at you, kid!" Augusta raised her glass and drank. "As long as necessary, I guess, or until my mission's accomplished."

"And what, pray tell, might that be?"

She patted her milk mustache with her napkin and smiled. "I don't suppose Bud Abbott and that tubby little Costello man are still making those amusing pictures? And what about that skinny young singer . . . Frank something or other? Oh, the girls used to swoon over him! 'The Voice,' they called him. Sang sweet enough to bring tears to a glass eye."

"Afraid not," I said. "And you didn't answer my question. Wasn't your mission accomplished when you kept me from hanging myself?"

"That wasn't my mission at all. I thought I explained that. If you had really meant to kill yourself, I wouldn't have been able to stop you."

"Then what?"

"Time will tell. Maybe it has something to do with the way your aunt died. Or the way you choose to live—

14

or should I say *exist?* For heaven's sake, Mary George, don't you *want* to find out what happened here?"

"Of course I do, but I can't imagine why anybody would want to hurt Aunt Caroline. She was the sweetest, kindest person I've ever known."

Augusta nodded. "And that's exactly why we'd want to put things right. Now, when was the last time you spoke with her?"

"Must've been a couple of weeks ago. I usually call . . . called every week, but with that mess at the office, and then Todd, I let it get by me . . . Didn't want her to worry." I stared at the lump of cake on my plate and pushed it away. I wasn't so hungry after all. Come to think of it, it was a week ago today my chicken-livered fiancé had left his sorry-to-hurt-you message on my answering machine. *One week ago*. And they had buried my aunt only yesterday.

"Do you remember what she said?" Augusta went to the window where she held aside the blue-flowered curtain to watch passing traffic. "My goodness!" she said, her eyes widening.

"Nothing special," I answered. "She was expecting her bridge club this week—today, in fact, and said she was giving the living room a thorough cleaning." That was when Aunt Caroline had found that old picture of Sam and me at the Easter-egg hunt. I smiled, remembering how my aunt always covered her dress in a huge red striped apron and tied her curly gray hair in a rag before attacking the enemy: dirt.

"And she'd been to see Dr. Kiker; he's our family doctor."

Augusta dropped the curtain and whirled about. "Ah!" she said. "So your aunt was in poor health?"

"Nothing that couldn't be controlled. High blood

15

pressure—sometimes she had dizzy spells. That's why I didn't want her in the attic, but she was on medication." I swallowed to keep my voice from shaking. "My aunt was only in her midsixties, she should've had a lot of years left. Dr. Kiker thinks she must've forgotten to take her medicine and had one of her swimmy-headed turns, but I think he's full of beans!" I stood abruptly, scraped my plate in the sink, and switched on the garbage disposal.

I heard the legs of a chair skidding across the floor behind me, and then a soft thud, followed by Augusta's frightened shriek. "What on earth are you doing under the table?" I asked.

"Get down!" Augusta yelled. "We're being blitzed!"

"It's only a garbage disposal." I reached out to her. "Come on, I'll show you how it works."

But Augusta held back. "Does it always come on like gangbusters? I thought we were being attacked." The woman straightened her pert hat, which didn't seem to have suffered from her dive under the table, and smoothed the frilly collar of her blouse. Angel or not, she really was quite vain. "I don't suppose you've looked up there yet?" Augusta said.

"Where?"

"In the attic. Look, maybe somebody gave your aunt a push, maybe not, but there must have been a reason she was taking a chance on those stairs. Something important. Maybe we can find out what it was." Augusta waited for me by the kitchen door. "Well? Come on, then."

And bossy too, I thought as I followed her up the narrow stairs.

It didn't take long to figure out somebody had been there before us.

I hadn't been in the attic since the week after Christmas when I came here to put away tree decorations, and at first I thought it looked much as I'd left it.

Except for the ceramic dog. The cookie jar with the chipped ear that always sat by the kitchen window. Aunt Caroline kept it filled with molasses crisps and snicker doodles, and I had broken the lid when I was about nine. But after I left home to take that job in Charlotte, my aunt didn't bake much anymore, and the ceramic dog was banished to the attic.

Now it sat in the middle of the floor in a box that once held the coffee maker I gave my aunt for her birthday. Gently I touched the top of its glossy head. Most of these things could be disposed of at a yard sale, but this I meant to keep. Just behind it to the left, a fold of yellowed lace cascaded from the trunk Aunt Caroline's mother had taken to college. It looked as though someone had dropped the lid in a hurry, leaving the contents in a tumble, and when I opened it, that's exactly what I found. Fringed shawls and satin slippers, lace-trimmed dainties, and the quaint cloche hats I'd loved to dress up in were tossed about as if somebody had wadded them up and thrown them there. The musty smell stung my nose.

"Would you look at this! I used to have a pair just like them!" Augusta snatched up a wrinkled pair of kid gloves the color of weak tea. Digging into the jumble she found a shimmering Champagne-colored dress with beaded flounces, which she held to the light. "Looks just about my size. This flapper style makes your hips look trim, don't you think?"

I didn't answer. I had moved on to a box of sheet music my aunt used to play at weddings. Somebody had stuffed it there in a hodgepodge with dog-eared edges,

17

and I didn't think it had been Aunt Caroline.

"Somebody's been up here," I said, but Augusta was too occupied with other things to pay attention. Now she twirled about the attic flapping an ostrich plume fan and humming an unfamiliar tune. "Aunt Caroline wouldn't have left her mother's trunk in such a mess," I said as she floated by, "and what's this?" Inside a garment bag thrown over an upturned chair, I found the wedding dress my aunt usually kept in the big oak wardrobe at the far end of the attic.

"I know it's out of style," Aunt Caroline had said, "but if you ever want to wear it, you know it would make me happy." I had tried it on when I was twelve and could barely get it buttoned. It couldn't be larger than a size six—probably perfect for Todd's new sexpot girlfriend. It would make me happy, I thought, if I could just fit into it.

I smoothed the rumpled dress and hung it back in the wardrobe, looking about to see if anything else was out of place, then turned to find Augusta Goodnight standing beside me. I hadn't even heard her cross the room—which in those heavy shoes was something of an accomplishment.

"Seems as though somebody was looking for something," Augusta said. "Do you think it could be the same person responsible for your aunt's death?"

"But what would they be looking for? She didn't have anything valuable, and she was still wearing her watch and rings when they found her." I moved a stack of old textbooks from a rickety ladder-back chair and sat, past worrying over dust and white pants. What kind of person would want to hurt Aunt Caroline? I didn't want it to be true. Surely my aunt's death had been an accident!

"Maybe she was interrupted while she was up here," I said. "The phone rang, or somebody came to the door. That might be why she left it this way. She meant to come back."

"But wouldn't she have left the lid to the trunk open? And what about that box of music? That's no way to go through sheet music."

Augusta had a point. Whoever had been here hadn't exactly turned the place upside down, but there were signs enough to tell me all wasn't right.

Augusta whisked dainty hands together and flicked invisible dust from her sleeve. "A bit grimy up here, isn't it?" She frowned at the small window curtained with cobwebs. "Rather gray and glum."

I grinned. "Grisly, grimy, glumpy bats . . ."

"I beg your pardon?" Augusta arched a perfect brow.

" 'Grisly, grimy, glumpy bats, brewed and stewed in lizard fat!' " I giggled. "It's a verse we made up at Summerwood. Now, what made me think of that?" Sam again. He could still make me laugh after almost twenty years.

It had rained earlier and the attic was steamy. I pushed a clinging strand of hair from my face and fanned myself with a program from a long-ago concert. If only I knew what I was looking for! "Why don't you check that end of the attic and see what turns up?" I said. "I'll look over here."

"Roger," Augusta Goodnight said.

I lasted about an hour. My shirt stuck to my back, my eyes itched from the dust, and I had tied an old bandana around my head to keep from looking like Medusa. If anyone had been here searching for something, I didn't know what it could have been.

19

Augusta, knee-deep in dusty cartons and humming sweetly, looked immaculate. "You're not planning to go out like that, are you?" she asked, glancing at me over her shoulder.

"Was I supposed to be going somewhere?"

"The shoe store. Remember? You did say you'd drive me to get some shoes this afternoon." Augusta eyed me critically. "I hope you're not going dressed like Rosie the Riveter."

Who on earth was Rosie the Riveter? I decided to let that pass. Had this curious person adopted me or something? How was I going to get rid of her? "I had planned to shower and change if it's quite all right with you," I told her. "Unless, of course, you're in some particular hurry."

Apparently sarcasm was lost on the woman. "I've waited fifty years to dump these dreadful shoes," she said. "Another few minutes won't hurt."

But when I got out of the shower, Augusta Goodnight was gone.

# CHAPTER 3

WHEN I'D GOTTEN THE NEWS ABOUT AUNT CAROLINE'S death, I had thrown a few essentials into an overnight bag—just enough to get me through the funeral. I hadn't yet decided to do away with myself, but life hadn't been all that great for me lately, and I didn't look forward to more of the same. I couldn't plan far enough ahead to pack.

Now, going through the closet in my old room, I found a rose-splashed cotton print I'd almost forgotten. I had left it there in September along with other lightweight clothing, and although it was only the beginning of May, it was plenty warm enough to wear it in Troublesome Creek, North Carolina. I wiggled bare clean toes into a pair of old sandals and sat on the bed to fasten them. I had chosen the daisy-sprigged bedspread with curtains to match when I was in high school, and my one-eyed teddy bear, a gift from Uncle Henry, sagged forlornly on the pillow. I gave him a fond squeeze. An hour or so ago I had thought I'd never enter this room again, never do the ordinary things like deciding what to wear. Now it seemed I would, at least for a little while longer, but how would I manage to get along without Aunt Caroline? She was always there when I needed her: steady and wise and comforting. Yet, except in the case of Todd Burkholder, she never offered advice unless I asked for it. If I could, I would ask for it now. What was I supposed to do? Where should I begin?

A list of course. Aunt Caroline always began with a list.

I was searching my desk drawer for pencil and paper when I came across the frog. Well, it's really not a frog, but a rock shaped like one. A "good-luck frog," my friend Sam had called it when he gave it to me the night before he left Summerwood. Painted green with brown spots and gold eyes that looked slightly crossed, it would keep me from being lonesome, Sam said. Only it didn't. When Sam told me good-bye that night at Summerwood, I knew I had lost my best friend. He was the first person near my age who showed me any kindness when my parents died, and the only one I could trust.

I set the frog on my dresser while I brushed my clean brown hair that smelled of Aunt Caroline's apricot

21

herbal shampoo. Feeling oddly relaxed, I fastened it back from my face and added a dab of lipstick, a slight smear of blush. I really needed a haircut, but haircuts cost money, and I didn't even have a job anymore.

A wren fidgeted in the camellia bush outside my window, but the house seemed hollow in its silence. Had this strange woman walked away, first helping herself to the family silver? Was she waiting for me behind the folding door to the dining room with Aunt Caroline's butcher knife? I walked through the empty rooms calling her name and was surprised at how disappointed I was when Augusta Goodnight didn't answer. Whoever she was, the woman had probably moved on to the next naive person who would supply her with chocolate cake and coffee. And a good laugh.

The living room looked as it always had—worn but comfortable, only my aunt wasn't in it. I ran a finger through the dust on the piano. If she could see it, Aunt Caroline would have a fit and fall in it! I grabbed a few tissues from the box on the end table and wiped it sort of clean. The mystery my aunt had been reading, one of Carolyn Hart's latest, was beside her chair with an envelope marking the place. I looked at the handwriting and saw that it was a note from me—to let my aunt know I'd be here for Mother's Day. I hadn't told her yet about that sewage sludge Todd Burkholder, or about the problems at work. And now I was glad.

I wish I could feel comforted in this place where Aunt Caroline had waited for me after school, tried patiently to teach me to play the piano, read aloud from *Heidi* and *Pinocchio* on rainy afternoons. It was the only home I could remember, but all I could feel was hurt. There was no one left for me. Uncle Henry and Aunt Caroline were gone, and the friends I'd known in school here had either moved away or started families of their own. I was alone. Losing my parents so early had made it hard for me to relate to others my own age, and I guess it carried over into adulthood. I was afraid to reach out, afraid to risk being hurt. Again.

I wasn't going to cry. Delia Sims. I would go over and talk with our neighbor. Augusta had advised me to get an appraisal on the furniture. At least she'd said one thing that made sense. I grabbed my keys and locked the door behind me—wondering if it would keep out angels—then headed across the street. That was when I noticed the frilly do-nothing hat atop the bright blob of hair atop the head in the passenger window of my car.

"What took you so long?" Augusta Goodnight wanted to know. "I've been sitting here so long, Kilroy came and went, then came back with his grandchildren."

"Kilroy?" I frowned at her, then laughed. I hadn't meant to laugh. Talk about annoying . . . meddlesome . . . add presumptuous to that! Who did she think she was?

"The shoes," Augusta reminded me. "We were going to shop for shoes." Then, "You look nice in that dress."

"Thank you." I got in beside her. Maybe I could dump her at the shoe store and scram.

But that was not to be. "I don't believe I've ever seen as much traffic!" Augusta held to her hat as though she thought it might blow away. "Where do all these cars come from?" It was hard for her to believe some families had two or three vehicles in the garage. *And* the gas to run them on. "And they're all going so fast! My, when I was here last, they wouldn't allow you to drive over thirty-five miles an hour."

We drove past the gray stone church where my aunt had belonged, and her parents and grandparents before her. Farther down the street the red-brick middle school,

23

abandoned now for a state-of-the-art building, seemed to mock us with its silence; weeds shoved through cracks in the cement walk, letters were missing from the sign out front. When my aunt subbed for the chorus teacher during my student days here, she'd pretended not to know me and I was secretly relieved. She knew how easily embarrassed kids are at that age, but it shamed me now to think of it.

I pulled into a parking space right in front of Hobgood's Bootery, just off the main street of town. "If you don't see anything you like in here," I said, "we'll have to go to the mall."

"The what?" Augusta made a face as she got out of the car. "Looks like I'll need some stockings too. This one has a ladder clear to my toes." She studied the display in the window and pointed to a pair of shoes. "I'll take those gold ones right there in a six double-A if they have them. Can't remember my stocking size."

"Never mind, we can guess," I said, heading for the entrance. "Well, come on, let's get it over with."

But Augusta shook her head. "You go on in, I'll wait." She gave me ten dollars from her handbag. "Will this be enough?"

"For a down payment maybe." Was she kidding? "Look at the price in the window. You have expensive taste."

"*Sixty dollars* for a pair of shoes! My heavens, do I took like Rockefeller?" Augusta positively swooned. "See what you can do for forty—and not a cent more!"

Chick Hobgood, the shop's proprietor and this afternoon's only clerk, hurried to offer his hand and his sympathy. "Your aunt and I went to school together, you know. She was only a couple of grades ahead of me." He shook his head. "Her accident was a shock to

24

us all."

I wanted to tell him my aunt's death was no accident and ask if he knew of any enemies she might have, but this wasn't the time. Instead I thanked him and selected some panty hose and a pair of shoes on sale that were as close as I could find to the ones in the window.

"Have you decided what you're going to do with the house, Mary George?" he asked, making change.

"Guess I'll have to sell it."

Mr. Hobgood smiled at me. "Didn't suppose you'd want to move back home now." He seemed disappointed.

"Actually I am looking for another job." Now, what made me tell him that? I took the change and watched him put my purchases in a bag with the familiar red lettering. Aunt Caroline had bought my first pair of heels in this same store.

He held on to the sack so long I thought I might have to pry it from him. "You might not be interested in this," he said, finally letting go, "but I hear Doc Nichols is looking for a receptionist. Last one quit after she had her baby."

"Doc Nichols?" I couldn't remember any doctor named Nichols.

Chick Hobgood laughed. "Animal doctor. Clarence Nichols is a veterinarian. Clinic's over on Elderberry Road—you know, where the old post office used to be."

I knew, and I thanked him. I would keep it in mind, I said.

It wasn't until I showed Augusta the shoes that I realized in my hurry I'd grabbed the wrong size. "Wait a minute—these are five triple-A's." I started to put them back in the bag. "Sorry. I'll run in and swap them, won't take a minute."

25

But Augusta already had them out of the box and on her feet. "Never mind, they'll do just fine," she said, holding them out in front of her.

"But they'll hurt your feet. Augusta, there's no way you can wear those shoes. Here, let me—"

"Honestly, there's plenty of room, see?" She easily slipped one off and on, her smile as pleased as a child's.

"Suit yourself," I said, hoping she wouldn't regret the choice. Some people push vanity to the limits!

But Augusta loved the shoes, marveled over the panty hose—"What? No garters?"—and hummed her exasperating tune all the way home. She disappeared to try on the hose as soon as we stepped inside, while I phoned my neighbor to thank her for the cake and ask about the furniture.

Not only had my aunt and Delia Sims grown up together but they'd been best friends and neighbors for years. When Aunt Caroline was president of the Women's Club, Delia was her vice president, and when Delia headed the Presbyterian Women, my aunt faithfully took the minutes.

"Oh, honey, I wish you didn't have to go through this right now." Delia spoke with a catch in her voice. "Some of your aunt's things you might want to keep. I wouldn't rush into anything just yet."

"Miss Delia, I really don't have any choice." It was hard to admit what an awful fix I was in, even to someone I knew as well as our neighbor, but I explained the situation without going into all the grim details.

There was silence on the line, and then a couple of dainty sniffs. "Well, bless your heart," Miss Delia said. "I'll just come over there this very afternoon and we'll go through that house. Give me a minute or so to feed these hungry kitties of mine, and I'll be right there."

And before I could answer, my neighbor had hung up.

*This very afternoon . . . I'll be right there.* As in now. I raced from room to room flapping at the dustiest places with a towel, and quickly rinsed the dishes in the sink. Someone had brought poppyseed muffins on a dainty, rose-patterned platter. I'd nibbled one for breakfast the day before and found it stale. Now I dumped the rest of the muffins down the disposal and quickly washed the plate, adding it to the stack to be returned. Now for the bathroom! Had I left dirty clothes on the floor after my shower? Probably, and my bedroom was a mess. And where was Augusta Goodnight? Waiting in the car again? Well, she could just wait!

In the waste basket in my bedroom I found two seamed stockings with runs, two worn circles of elastic, and a pair of very ugly shoes. But no Augusta Goodnight. I felt slightly used. I had fed this strange creature, chauffeured her about, and now I'd been abandoned. Well, good riddance! In the front hall I heard Miss Delia's soft little owl call, "Ouu-oo?" and hurried to greet her.

Having shed her clumsy shoes, the woman calling herself Augusta apparently had taken off again just as I began to wonder if I really could help bring my aunt's killer to justice. *Somebody* had to, didn't they? And now it looked as though I'd have to do it myself. Angel, my foot! Still, I found myself humming that annoying song of Augusta's while Delia prowled the dining room.

. "My goodness, that old song brings back memories!" Delia Sims pulled her head from inside the dark oak sideboard. "Haven't heard that old thing in years. Where in the world did you hear it?"

"That? I don't know. It just kind of stuck in my head.

27

Must've heard it on the radio." I glanced over my shoulder, half expecting to see Augusta Goodnight standing behind me with a disapproving look. I could sense her discomfort when I lied. But she wasn't there. "What's the name of it?" I asked. "Do you remember?"

"Of course," Delia said. "It was popular back in the forties during World War Two. It's called 'Coming in on a Wing and a Prayer.' "

I smiled and turned away. "That figures," I whispered to no one at all.

# CHAPTER 4

THE LETTER CAME THE NEXT DAY. LESS THAN forty-eight hours after my aunt's funeral I received an envelope addressed to me in her round, hurried scrawl, and my body went rag-doll limp as I ripped it open. How wonderful to imagine that Aunt Caroline wasn't dead! It had all been a ghastly mistake, and someone else was buried in that plot on the side of the hill behind Cleveland Avenue Presbyterian Church. After all, wasn't she writing to me as always?

Only the letter had been forwarded from my Charlotte address, and the postmark was over a week old. I took the tissue-thin pages into the living room so I couldn't see the stairs where she fell, and read through a hot film of tears. The letter was dated four days before she died:

> *Mary George honey!*
> Wish you'd stay at home once in a while! I've tried to phone three times.
> Guess what? Remember that old Bible you

28

brought with you as a child? Well, I ran across it while dusting the bookshelves the other day—the day after I found that cute picture of you and the little boy at the Easter-egg hunt. (Sam, wasn't it? You used to talk about him all the time). Anyway, the Bible had fallen behind that set of encyclopedias, and no telling how long it's been there—which should give you an idea of how lax I've become about dusting, or about looking things up, for that matter!

At any rate I think I've discovered something that might lead to exciting news—at least I hope it will. I'll tell you about it when you come for Mother's Day.

Can hardly wait to see you! Am trying hard to lose weight, but just this once I'll bake us something special. What about a strawberry shortcake? That was always your favorite.

By the way, I'm holding off announcing your engagement in the paper here until I hear from you. It's not too late to change your mind, you know. And Delia tells me several of the churches there in Charlotte have active singles groups!??!

*Much love as ever from your*
*aunt Caroline*


I smiled. My aunt never did take to the idea of my marrying Todd. The one time I brought him home with me he came to the dinner table wearing a baseball cap, and to top it all, never wrote a proper thank-you note. Maybe I should've picked up on that. Good raising will always tell, Aunt Caroline said.

I folded the pages into a tiny square and tucked them

29

into my bra as I sat in her rocking chair, my hands on the worn arms where her hands had been. This was as close as I was ever going to get to the woman who raised me, and I felt hollow inside without her.

Later, when Delia came over to help me sort my aunt's belongings, I showed the letter to her as we wrapped Aunt Caroline's fragile, fern-patterned china, her crystal stemware, and packed them in boxes. For me, my neighbor insisted, because my aunt would want me to use it, pass it on.

But pass it on to whom? I thought, picturing (with relief) a baby with Todd Burkholder's big ears, wearing a baseball cap.

"Did Aunt Caroline ever mention that Bible to you?" I asked.

Delia shook her head silently as she read the note, then wiped her eyes with the hem of her apron. "No, but then I was in Atlanta for over a week during Doreen's surgery—had that by-pass thing. Doreen's my only sister, only sibling, really. We lost our little brother when he was just a child." She looked at the letter again. "I expect she ran across your Bible while I was away."

"Wonder what she meant by, 'something that could lead to exciting news,' " I said. I couldn't imagine anything exciting in my family background.

"Why don't you look and see? Where is the Bible? Maybe we can find out." Delia ran a finger around the rim of a goblet. It made a clear, ringing sound.

"That's just it, I can't find it. I've looked in her desk, the table by her bed, all the likely places."

"Must've put it somewhere for safekeeping," Delia said. "It's bound to turn up when we start going through the books."

But it didn't. Aunt Caroline had put away the Bible

soon after I came to live here. It was old, she said, and the pages were thin. I was given a sturdier, modern translation that was still in the stand next to my bed in my two-room Charlotte apartment, or it was the last time I looked. I've sort of gotten out of the habit of reading it, I'm afraid.

The old family edition I'd brought with me to Snapfinger Road had a place of honor on the bookshelf in the living room until, somehow or other, it must have slipped behind the row of bulky reference books.

I didn't find the Bible in the tall, glassed-in case in the back hall, or in any of the numerous stacks of "books to be read" that had accumulated around the house. I even checked my aunt's "secret" places where she used to hide my Christmas gifts in a crevice behind her closet shelf, or buried in her lingerie drawer. Nothing. Again I searched the shelves in the living room. No luck there either.

"Delia, have you noticed anybody unusual over here lately?" I asked as we emptied the kitchen cabinets.

She examined a rusting sifter and tossed it aside. "What do you mean *unusual*?"

"Somebody you didn't know. Somebody who . . . well, maybe shouldn't have been here."

"Well, other than the usual folks, Bonita Moody's the only person I've seen on a regular basis. Now, *she's* peculiar—but probably not in the way you mean." Delia looked at me through narrowed eyes. "Mary George, why are you asking me this? Surely you don't think somebody was responsible for Caroline's death!"

"I don't know," I said. "I'm just asking." But I did know. I knew somebody had killed my aunt just as surely as I was standing there on her worn blue linoleum with a chipped brown pitcher in my hand, but I didn't

31

want to frighten Delia.

I put the pitcher aside with the sifter. "Who's Bonita Moody? What do you know about her?"

"Not much to know. Late thirties maybe, cashier at the Triple Value—you know, that new mart where the feed store used to be. I've noticed her over here several times. Rabbity little thing. Acts like she'd wet her pants if you said boo."

"When was she usually here?" I asked.

"Monday afternoons as a rule, about the middle of the day. Always parked in back. I'd see her turning in when I came out to get my mail."

"Did Aunt Caroline ever mention her?"

Delia looked at me strangely. "I never asked, Mary George. Just figured she must've been helping with some of the heavy cleaning. Caroline wasn't up to it with her blood pressure and all. 'Course, she'd never admit it to me. Your aunt didn't tell me everything, you know."

Did I detect a bit of resentment there? "Do you remember if she was here the day Aunt Caroline died?" I asked.

"That would be on a Tuesday, so I doubt it—no, wait! That was the day I took the kitties to the vet for their leukemia shots, and I saw her turning in as I backed out of the driveway. I remember wondering why she was coming on a different day. You know, Mary George, I believe she was here."

"Did you see Aunt Caroline after she left?"

Delia sat abruptly and propped her head in her hands. She reminded me of the illustrations in nursery rhyme books with her dainty Mother Goose face and white hair pulled back in a neat bun. And when she stood her head came barely to my chin. Now she looked like a little old child sitting there and it made my heart turn over. "I don't remember . . . I honestly don't remember! Mary George, is this important? Do you really think that woman had anything to do with Caroline's fall?"

I could see I was upsetting her, and I really felt awful about it, but I had to know. "I'm not sure she fell," I said.

I got one of those silent, sympathetic looks people reserve for friends who are going off the deep end. Yet I could tell she was holding something back.

"Was there anyone else?" I asked softly.

Delia shrugged. "Well, it's been a while, but there was a man—young fellow. He was here several times back in the early spring. I teased Caroline about him once. Kind of embarrassed her, I think. I could tell she didn't want to talk about it."

"When's the last time you saw him?" I asked.

She rose and began wrapping the last of the mismatched dinner plates. "Oh, dear, I don't know. Several weeks at least. I just knew I'd never seen him before, haven't seen him since."

She sighed. "Whoever he was, your aunt Caroline wasn't telling."

I set my aunt's cookbook aside to keep. One of these days I might even learn to use it. "She seemed to be looking forward to having her bridge club over," I said. The group had been playing together for years.

Delia nodded sadly. "Not many of us left now. Folks just don't play anymore."

"She'd even circled the dessert she meant to serve—something with about a million calories with nuts and dates and whipped cream."

"Don't know why," Delia said. "Most of us are trying to lose weight. Told me she was going to have a minted fruit compote with some of those low-fat cookies." She sighed. "Everybody carries on so about cholesterol. Seems they've just taken all the fun out of eating!" And she pried open the lid of a cookie tin to see if there was anything inside.

There was. "Have one, please. Take some home," I offered. Everybody loved Aunt Caroline, and this was their way of showing it. People had brought more food than I could possibly eat, and other than the women from the church and a few neighbors who came over the day of the funeral, I'd had no one to share it.

Except for Augusta. And now, after bullying me to take her to the shoe store, the peculiar woman had disappeared. She was only here for an afternoon, yet it seemed she'd been a part of my life forever. If it weren't for the discarded shoes and stockings, I'd swear I had imagined her.

"Mm—lemon crinkles! Bess Hazelwood. She always makes 'em." Delia squinted at the name on the bottom of the container. "See, just like I said. But some people don't even bother to label things—have to be a mind reader to know who they belong to." She bit into another cookie. "I'll be glad to return these things when you're ready. After all this time, I've pretty much learned what goes where.

"Take that, for instance." My neighbor frowned at the empty pink-flowered plate. "Fronie Temple. Muffins, I'll bet."

I nodded.

"Banana nut or poppyseed?"

"Poppyseed." I tried not to make a face.

"Uh-huh. Left something out, didn't she? Fronie's bad about that. Gets in a hurry, you know. Why, she made a cake for the Women's Club bake sale last year,

34

must've weighed a ton. Forgot to put in the baking powder. 'Course nobody bought it."

Delia wrapped the last of Aunt Caroline's everyday plates and tucked them inside the box, giving it sort of a farewell pat. "Now, there's an idea," she said, retrieving the masking tape from under a stack of newspapers.

She looked so triumphant standing there with her bifocals askew and a smudge of ink on her cheek, it made me smile—until I remembered what we were doing and why.

"What?" I asked, just to be polite.

"Fronie Temple. She's had her house converted into apartments. Fellow who rented the one downstairs moved out last month, took a job in Raleigh. Hear she's looking for a new tenant."

Meaning me, I guess. "Hold on, I don't even have a job," I said.

"But you will, and you have to live someplace." She seemed dead set on me moving to Troublesome Creek, and now that I thought about it, a fresh start didn't seem like such a bad idea. "Of course you'd have to put up with Fronie's singing," she continued, "but if we can stand her screeching in the choir every Sunday, you can learn to get used to it. Be good for your constitution. Besides, it's an old house. Walls can't be too thin."

I groaned, picturing an old wreck of a house with a banshee for a landlady. Not an appealing prospect.

Delia labeled the box and shoved it aside, then sat with a tired little moan. "You know I'd like to have you myself, Mary George, but to tell the truth, I don't plan to be here long either. That old elephant of a house is too much to keep up, and I don't need all that room anyway. Joy Ellen lives so far away, she hardly ever gets home anymore."

Joy Ellen was Delia's daughter, an only child who lives somewhere in California. I knew from Aunt Caroline she'd tried to get Delia to move out there, but North Carolina was her home, our neighbor said, and this was where she meant to stay.

"Where will you go?" I asked.

"Been looking at those condominiums they're building out on Pine Thicket Road," Delia told me. "They're especially for retired people, you know—easy to keep and all. I should be able to move in by late summer if I can unload that old place of mine." She went to the sink for water. "You might want to call Fronie, though, let her know you're interested."

Oh, but I wasn't. "She's probably rented it already."

"Not unless somebody's taken it since I saw her in Anderson's Market this morning. Asked me if I knew anybody who'd be interested." She laughed. "Must be gettin' plumb featherheaded! Didn't even think of you till now, Mary George." Delia darted me a look. "It's right close by. Air-conditioned too. I'll go with you to see it if you like."

She didn't want me to leave her. Leave Troublesome Creek. She had just lost her best friend, and Delia Sims was lonely. Well, I knew loneliness too. Besides, Delia Sims wasn't my problem. Didn't I have troubles enough of my own? "First let me see about a job," I said.

It was all happening too fast. The house and everything in it had to be disposed of. Now. And there was my apartment back in Charlotte to think about. I was being forced to make decisions I wasn't accustomed to making, and I didn't like it. Hot springs pooled behind my eyes. My breathing came too fast.

Then, for some reason, I thought of Augusta Goodnight with her new gold shoes and silly hat and a

36

soothing blue-green calmness washed over me. For a minute I was splashing in the cool creek back at Summerwood catching tapoles, building "frog houses" with bare feet on the sandy banks. With Sam.

Suddenly Delia, who had been sorting table linens, stopped and sniffed. "Don't tell me, " she said. "Darcy Fuller brought her strawberry pie."

I shook my head. I'd know it if somebody had brought strawberry pie.

She frowned. "Shortcake?"

"Nope. Sorry."

I could tell she didn't believe me. "Well, that's the strangest thing. I can smell it right here in this kitchen, just as plain as day." Delia took a deep breath. "Mm! Whatever it is, it's heavenly."

"Absolutely, I said.

# CHAPTER 5

I FELL IN LOVE THE MINUTE I SAW HIM. HE HAD HAIR the color of November woods and eyes that turned me into marshmallow creme. I knew we belonged to each other.

He raised his head and looked at me. He knew. And when I knelt beside him, he licked my hand—all the way to the elbow, his long tail thumped the floor.

"What happened?" I said to the boy who held the dog by a piece of rope.

"Cut his paw pretty bad on something, and he ain't eatin' neither." The boy stroked the dog's big, shaggy head. He looked worried.

I noticed the dirty, crusted wound on the left forepaw, the matted fur. My new love smelled like a sewer from hell. "What's his name?"

"Don't know. Granddaddy says somebody must've dumped him out and left him. I was supposed to take him to the pound, but thought I'd try here first. He's a good old dog. Maybe Doc Nichols knows somebody who'll take him."

"You did the right thing." I remembered what it was like being "dumped" in a strange place.

I had $149.74 in my checking account, no job, and a house being sold out from under me. "I'll take him," I said.

The waiting room smelled of disinfectant and dogs, and the woman behind the receptionist's counter looked at her watch at least three times while I waited to see the vet. "Gotta drive carpool in ten minutes," she explained to the balding man with a wheezing dachshund. "School lets out at three o'clock." Later I found out she was Doc Nichols's sister filling in for a day. When a reluctant teenaged boy was called from cleaning cages in the back to take her place at the desk, I knew the job was mine.

"When can you start?" Doc Nichols said.

Clarence Nichols was almost as tall as the doorframe and thin enough to slip through a crack. I could tell his curly hair used to be red, and his eyes were as blue as those picture postcards other people send me of the Caribbean. We talked for almost an hour while he cleaned the teeth of a couple of anesthetized cats and trimmed the nails of a cocker spaniel. He called me Sport because of my initials, M. G., which is about as close to a sports car as I'll probably ever come. But I liked it—and him. Nobody's ever called me Sport before.

The hairy brown dog, a mix, he said, of God knows

what, turned out to be a puppy. Maybe six months old, the doctor told me, no more. Besides the cut on his foot, the animal was anemic, needed worming, and fleas had established a summer resort in his coat.

Doc Nichols examined the injured paw and frowned. "Poor baby's been through a lot. It would be the kindest thing, I suppose, to—"

"No! I want him," I said. "He's mine." I named him Hairy Brown.

"You have a *what*?" Delia put down her account book and shoved her glasses back in place.

"A dog," I said. "But don't worry, he's staying at the vet's until I can get settled." Doc Nichols was only charging me for the vitamin shots and medicine.

"Oh, dear. I don't know if Fronie allows animals," Delia said.

Then I'd just have to live in a tent. Right now I didn't have time to worry about it. The few pieces of Aunt Caroline's furniture I'd decided to keep had been tagged for delivery to the small three-room apartment in the rear of Fronie Temple's house, along with the things I'd recently hauled from my—now empty—apartment in Charlotte. Thanks to Delia's experience in the trade, an antiques dealer was due to collect my aunt's dining room furniture and the huge Victorian bed that had belonged to her grandmother. The rest, priced to sell and displayed, warts and all, in the house on Snapfinger Road, would go up for grabs to whoever wanted it at eight o'clock the next morning.

Everywhere I looked were the worn, familiar things of home. Aunt Caroline's shabby sofa—the one she'd covered herself—the lamp Uncle Henry made from a crockery jug, faded prints that hung in the hall.

39

I'd kept my aunt's sewing basket, her bisque figurines, even the fraying needlepoint footstool with the wobbly leg—things I couldn't bear to part with. Add to that the bookshelves, drop-leaf table, and Windsor chair I'd bought on time. Where would I put them all? But despite continued searching, my old family Bible had failed to turn up. I wished I could share Delia's confidence that it would eventually resurface among the books I'd packed to keep.

That afternoon the real estate agent called to tell me he'd had an offer on the house. "Couple of attorneys plan to convert it into offices," he said. "Better take it," the agent advised. "Offers aren't pouring in. Besides, this whole neighborhood's in a transitional zone."

Taking Delia's advice, I told him to accept the offer, then called and invited my neighbor out for hamburgers. Not so much to celebrate—I really didn't feel like celebrating—but if the sale went through, at least I would be able to pay off some of my aunt's debts. And I had to get away from this house! Suddenly my life was in fast-forward, and the only way I could deal with it was to pretend, for a little while at least, that it wasn't happening.

The Hound Dog Café, which offers fifties tunes on a jukebox and the best sandwiches in town, was understandably crowded since there aren't that many places to eat in Troublesome Creek, North Carolina, and we had to wait for a booth.

"Do you want to get something from the take-out window?" I asked Delia. She looked tired and pretty close to her age, which is sixty-eight. "We can eat at home if you like."

"Not on your life," she said. "I'm tired of looking at the same walls. Besides," she whispered, "it'll give me

40

time to run in the rest room a minute. Why don't you play us a tune on the jukebox while we wait?"

Delia disappeared behind the pink door stenciled in even pinker lips and I shoved a couple of quarters into the slot and punched up "Blue Suede Shoes." Maybe Elvis would revive my sagging energy.

A booth emptied a few minutes later, so I grabbed it and listened to the music while trying to ignore the clutter of somebody else's meal. As a waitress in pink hair bows cleared the table, I thought of Augusta dancing in the attic and wondered where she was. A pity she'd missed out on the era of rock and roll.

If Augusta Goodnight were really my guardian angel, I thought, she'd better get her heavenly body back here where she belonged. I had a feeling I was going to need her. And what was she really here for? Would Augusta leave for good after we learned how Aunt Caroline died?

I looked at the people sitting about me—talking, laughing, pigging out on burgers and fries. They all seemed harmless enough, but if someone really had pushed Aunt Caroline down the attic stairs, what was to stop them from coming after me?

I don't know how long the song had been playing before I realized what it was. It certainly wasn't "Blue Suede Shoes." Of course! How could I forget? The old forties song, "Coming in on a Wing and a Prayer," was playing over the jukebox, and no one seemed to have noticed it but me.

"Do you hear that?" I asked the waitress.

She rolled her eyes. "What? 'Blue Suede Shoes'? I hear it in my sleep!"

When Delia returned, the song had just finished playing. "Did you hear it?" I asked. "That song you

41

were telling me about, the one popular during the war."

She studied the menu. "Couldn't hear much of anything back there. Besides, that's the wrong decade, isn't it?"

"But it played. I heard it. It has to be on the jukebox." I ran a finger down the selections, checked the list three times. The song wasn't there.

That night I slept for the last time in the house on Snapfinger Road. The next day, as soon as the sale was over, several teens from Aunt Caroline's church would haul my belongings to Fronie Temple's in the back of a pickup truck. Most had been in my aunt's children's choir since nursery school age and wouldn't accept a cent in payment for helping me, so I planned to make a donation to their youth group in her memory. Aunt Caroline would like that.

"Your aunt always made me feel important, that my voice counted," Becky Wainwright told me. Becky was tall and shy and didn't have much to say, but her mellow contralto could knock you off your feet, and I'd heard she'd won honors in several choral competitions. Still, as much as I needed it, I felt a little guilty about accepting volunteer help.

"Now, don't you worry a minute about that," Miss Fronie said the next morning as she browsed among the jumble in what used to be Uncle Henry's study. "Your aunt Caroline spent every Sunday since I can remember playing for that congregation—not to mention the time she put in with all those children, and for our Wednesday night choir practice."

Fronie Temple leafed through a worn copy of *Wuthering Heights,* set it aside. "We're sure going to miss her," she said. "Your aunt was so good to run through the anthems with me. Now, *she* appreciated a trained voice. I honestly don't know what we'll do without her," Miss Fronie stroked a brocaded pillow and turned away. "Some people just can't be replaced."

"I have something for you," I said, leading her into the dining room where boxes lined the floor. "I'm sure Aunt Caroline would have wanted you to have her sheet music." Every Wednesday night for as long as I could remember, Fronie Temple had driven my aunt to choir practice, pausing in front of the house with two light taps of her horn at precisely thirteen minutes after seven. Aunt Caroline had given up driving years before when, as a teen, she'd been involved in an accident, and Fronie had seemed glad of her company.

Fronie was so overcome by the gift she couldn't speak, but squeezed my arm in thanks. My new landlady was stout and sixtyish and tinted her hair baby-chicken yellow. I knew her slightly as I was growing up, but hadn't seen her in a while. From what I could see under the makeup, she once had beauty queen looks, and was trying to hang on to what remained the best way she knew how.

Aside from having to listen to the woman's tremorous soprano, maybe it wouldn't be so bad living in the rear of Fronie Temple's house. After all, she was a friend of Aunt Caroline's.

Fronie didn't know many people in town when she moved here after marrying Braswell Temple, my aunt had said, and Aunt Caroline sort of took her under her wing: invited her to join the Women's Club, tried to make her feel welcome. I left her thumbing through the music and spent the next few minutes selling casette tapes I'd collected in high school to a middle-aged man in a flower-splashed shirt.

They paraded through all morning. The young mother with twin girls bought Aunt Caroline's portable sewing machine, and the portly man from Charlotte, Uncle Henry's collection of *National Geographic*. A matronly woman with grandchildren in tow carried off a carton of children's books, minus my favorites, of course.

By the middle of the afternoon I was beginning to droop like a wilting petunia. The crowd had thinned, but a few scavengers still picked about the remains of my aunt's life. It hurt to see strangers walking away with familiar things she and my uncle had used. I had sold the last of the garden tools and was about to go inside for a cool drink when Delia tugged at my arm.

"There she is," she said, nodding toward a small, dark woman looking through a box of shoes.

"There who is?"

"Bonita Moody. That woman in the green dress— she's the one I told you about. She was here the day Caroline fell."

The woman hugged a navy handbag under one arm while a little boy about six clung to the other. Bonita Moody was examining a pair of my aunt's white pumps, the ones she bought on sale last summer, when she saw me approaching across the lawn. Then a couple of people stopped to ask me a question, and the next thing I knew she was gone.

How could she disappear so quickly? I looked all around but didn't see her, then, as I started back to the house, I glimpsed a flash of bright green. Bonita Moody and her little boy were getting into a car parked at the curb with a man behind the wheel. "Wait!" I yelled, hurrying after her, but the car sped away.

The child turned and waved to me as the old gray Chevrolet disappeared around the corner, but the

44

woman in it never looked back.

"She must have heard me calling. Why did she ignore me like that?" I asked Delia.

"Peculiar—like I told you," my neighbor said. "Belongs to one of those far-out religious sects. Thinks it's a sin to go to the bathroom."

"Wow! That must get pretty uncomfortable."

She laughed. "Well, you know what I mean."

That night we counted the proceeds. We had taken in a little over a thousand dollars, which, with the sale of the house and furniture, would enable me to pay off the rest of my aunt's funeral expenses and most of her other debts as well. Aunt Caroline had been forced to borrow a large chunk of money after Uncle Henry died, and had been repaying it by the month.

I was glad not only for Delia's bookkeeping skills but for her easygoing, practical nature, and I spent that night in her home. The next morning I moved into the box-crammed three-room apartment in the rear of Fronie Temple's faded brick house that sat back from the road in a tangle of dogwood and rhododendron. "I never did like to cut grass," my landlady said. "And I'm not about to start now!"

My belongings had been delivered the afternoon before, but other than the day I'd rented the apartment when the rooms were bare and fresh with paint, I hadn't had a chance to inspect what was to be my home.

Home. Aunt Caroline's favorite rocker, Uncle Henry's old leather chair, the china lamp with a hand-painted shade. Stacks of books. Dishes. Boxes of linens. Silence. And me.

The rooms were fairly large with high ceilings and a row of windows the one end of the living area. The walls had been painted a pale yellow by someone who wasn't too neat, and tiny drops and spatters dotted hardwood floors that probably hadn't been refinished since the house was built. It was much like the house I grew up in, and I should feel right at home. But I didn't. I was alone, tired, and surrounded by the biggest mess I'd ever seen. I sat on a packing crate and thought of all the things I had to do. My salary at the animal clinic wasn't as much as I'd been making in Charlotte, but the rent was less, and I might just get by if I didn't eat too much.

Still, I wasn't one step closer to finding out who murdered Aunt Caroline. I had a strong feeling it had something to do with the missing Bible, and I was determined to find it. How, I didn't know. I did know that if anything had happened to me, my aunt would have made it her business to learn who was responsible, and that I was letting her down. Suddenly I felt like the last person in the world, and grief, like a heavy, gray blanket settled about my shoulders. Tears swelled hot in my throat, and I cried until a kind numbness came over me. I felt empty. A rag doll with no stuffing.

"Feeling better now? A good cry usually helps, I think. But duty calls, Mary George. All these things aren't going to get put away by themselves." The words, spoken softly, were nevertheless emphatic, and I looked up and saw her there. Augusta Goodnight had traded her froufrou hat for a bright blue bandana and she stood in the kitchen doorway with a box of utensils—which she made a point of rattling. "Well, come on, let's get on with it! The kitchen first, don't you think?

"And what do you call this oven the size of a bread box? Does it really cook as fast as they claim?"

# CHAPTER 6

IT WAS ALMOST A WEEK BEFORE I REALIZED THE cookie jar was missing. To tell the truth, it took about that long to sort through the clutter and put everything away, especially with Augusta's help.

"A place for everything, and everything in its place," she told me, putting my curling iron in the silverware drawer. Thought it was a cooking utensil, I suppose. A few days later I discovered my pizza cutter in Uncle Henry's household toolbox. Looked like a lawn edger to her, Augusta said.

But, to give credit where it's due, it was Augusta who made me aware that the cookie jar was gone.

"You need something bright up here," she said as we lined the kitchen shelves with yellow scalloped paper. "Don't you have a flower pot or something? Maybe a big jar?"

I knew immediately what had happened. It was that awful, hopeless feeling you get when you know you've done something stupid and it's too late to do anything about it, like the second after you lock your keys in the car.

But we looked anyway. There were still a couple of boxes I hadn't unpacked, and I shifted the contents to the floor.

"Are you sure you didn't put it away someplace?" I asked Augusta. *Like in the refrigerator? The shower?* But it would be hard to hide anything as big as that china dog in three small rooms.

"Forget it," I said finally. "I'm afraid it's no use, it's gone. It must've been sold at the attic sale."

Augusta folded her arms. "Think," she said. Her tone,

I thought, had a most unangelic inflection. "When was the last time you saw it?"

I had labeled the box and set it aside back in Uncle Henry's study, but with all the confusion and people poking about, it could have been picked up by mistake. I sat on the floor and tried to remember who might have bought it. The frail little man who happily carted off that old clock that hadn't worked in years? The large woman in the T-shirt that said If Mama Ain't Happy, Ain't Nobody Happy? "Maybe Delia remembers," I said, tossing an assortment of unsold kitchen knickknacks back into the box to go to the next white-elephant sale.

Augusta, searching again under the sink for the missing jar, disappeared as usual when somebody knocked at the door.

"Mary George?" My landlady sang out. "I thought you might like a few slices of my rum cake for dessert tonight."

I still had half a bowl of potato salad she'd brought over a couple of days before. It tasted okay after I added a little onion and some mustard and pickles.

She stood on my doorstep with a covered plate in her hand, and the first sight of her jolted me as it always did. Her screaming purple lipstick went way over the edge of where her lips ought to be, and the color seemed to jump out at me. And then of course there's that Easter-chicken hair.

Her large bosom preceded her as I stepped back to let her inside. "Hope I'm not interrupting . . ." She looked about. "Thought I heard somebody talking in here."

"You did. Me." I smiled as I accepted the plate. "I've misplaced a favorite cookie jar and I'm afraid it was sold by mistake." I shrugged. "Must've been fussing to myself. You didn't see it, did you? A china dog with a broken ear?"

"Lord, honey, at my age I'm getting so forgetful, I wouldn't remember it if I had!" She shook her head. "Why, sometimes I go into a room and clean forget what I came for. Too much on my mind, I reckon, but I can't stand it if I'm not busy." With a long sigh, Fronie sank into Uncle Henry's brown leather chair and fanned herself with yesterday's paper.

I came close to asking about her policy on pets, but I just couldn't bring myself to do it. What if she said no? Hairy Brown was looking a lot better. His foot was healing well, and Doc Nichols said if his appetite got any better, I'd have to invest in a pet food company. I looked forward to bringing him home. Augusta was fickle about keeping me company, and it would be comforting having a dog around, especially at night.

"You don't mind if I sit a minute, do you? These old legs are about to give out on me. You've got it looking real nice in here, Mary George, but it sure seems strange seeing Caroline's things in a different place."

I brought her a cup of tea, and between swallows of Earl Grey, my landlady listed on one hand the things she had to do that day.

" . . . and sometimes I get migraines so bad I just have to lie down. I know I take on too many things, but then, somebody's got to do it . . ."

When she started counting on the other hand, I groped for another subject.

"Miss Fronie, do you know a woman named Bonita Moody?"

"Bonita Moody. Works over there at the Triple Value, doesn't she?"

"That's the one. Delia says she's seen her at Aunt

Caroline's a lot. And she was at the attic sale last week."

She drained her cup and nodded. "Piano student."

"What?"

"Bonita Moody. She was taking piano lessons from Caroline. Been studying for several months now, I think."

Then why did the woman act so strange and run away when I tried to approach her?

That night I dreamed I found the cookie jar. I was a child again back at the house on Snapfinger Road playing hide-and-seek with Sam. But that didn't make any sense because Sam left the children's home before I came to live in that house. But then dreams are usually mixed up anyway; in this one, I saw Sam running up the back stairs, heard his muffled laughter behind the closed attic door. But when I opened it, Sam was gone. The attic was bare except for the cookie jar, still in the box where I'd seen it the day Augusta came. Yet I knew there was nothing up there. Delia and I had checked twice.

Still, the next day I forced myself to go back inside that empty shell of a house. I had only moved out the week before, yet it had an air of being long abandoned. This house had been my home, my place of refuge, yet I felt uneasy here.

With Delia standing guard at the foot of the steps and Augusta hovering nearby, I went up those dark, musty stairs once more. But just as I thought, the cookie jar wasn't there.

"Didn't you say you first saw it in the middle of the attic floor, apart from everything else?" Augusta reminded me. "I believe your aunt may have been trying to tell you something."

50

"It seems to me if you really were an angel, you'd *know* what she meant, or at least where I could find it." I was hot and tired, and disgusted with myself for letting the cookie jar go, and the empty house made me sad. "What good is it being an angel," I said, "if you don't know any more than that?"

"Sorry," Augusta Goodnight said. "That's not in my job description."

But I realized she was right about the cookie jar. For whatever reason, the chipped ceramic dog was important, and somehow I had to find it.

"Do you suppose Bonita Moody might have bought it?" Delia asked later. "Remember? We saw her shopping around that day."

But surely I would have noticed it if she had been carrying something as bulky as that.

At any rate, it gave me an excuse to pay a visit to Bonita Moody. Face to face, maybe she would tell me about the last time she saw my aunt alive.

The Moodys, Delia told me, lived in Mimosa Village on the east side of town. I remembered the area as a checkerboard of small mill-owned houses built about sixty years ago. The cotton mill closed before I came to live here, and the houses are now privately owned. The Moodys' neat home was gray with white trim, and pink geraniums bloomed by the walk. A little girl about nine sat in the porch swing, but ran inside when she saw me. Was there something about me, or did skittishness run in the family?

Through the screen I looked into a narrow hall where a spray of magnolias sprang from a white pitcher on a table by the door. Their sweet perfume reminded me of the big tree by the dining room window back at Summerwood, and of Sam who always ate his dessert

51

first, and mine too if he could get it. In a singsong voice, the two of us would quote our disgusting verse about bats and lizards and worse to discourage others from wanting their cookies or cupcakes, or whatever Cookie reluctantly doled out. And for the first time in years I thought of Cindy, who had worked in the kitchen at Summerwood and who sometimes slipped us extra goodies. Smiling, I rang the bell.

She knew immediately who I was, and I knew immediately I wasn't welcome. I would have to talk fast before the door closed in my face.

"Those magnolias smell wonderful, and they look pretty in that vase." I smiled again, making no attempt to enter. Good. At least she was still there.

"I'm looking for a cookie jar," I said. "China dog with a chipped ear." I introduced myself. "I saw you at our attic sale last week and hoped you might've noticed who bought it."

Her tension eased slightly, but she still wasn't ready to invite me for Sunday dinner.

"It was special to me," I added. "Belonged to my aunt, and I'd really like to have it back."

With one hand, Bonita smoothed the collar of her blouse. "I didn't see it," she told me, shaking her head. "Ray—that's my husband—he was in a hurry to leave. Didn't have much of a chance to look around." She paused. "I'm real sorry about your aunt." The words were almost whispered.

"Thank you. I understand you took piano from her, and I wondered if you might have seen my aunt that day, right before she died."

If I had told her we were being invaded by machete-wielding Martians I don't think she could have freaked out more. She wheeled around as if she expected

52

Norman Bates himself to be lurking in the background. I felt a little jumpy myself.

"No, that's not true. I don't know where you heard that. I hardly knew your aunt."

*Whoa, now! Back up, lady, before you sink in any deeper,* I thought. Something was definitely wrong here. Her belligerent denial made me want to strike back. It was as if she had erased Aunt Caroline from her life, like my aunt didn't matter. Why was this woman lying to me?

"I'm sorry I bothered you," I muttered, then turned and walked away. I was halfway down the walk when she called to me.

"Mary George, wait! Look, I'm sorry. What I said back there wasn't true." With a hand on my arm, Bonita Moody walked with me to the curb where I'd parked my car. Her voice was so low I walked bending over to hear her.

"It's Ray, you see. He didn't want me taking those lessons. Says we can't afford them." She looked back at the house and sighed. "Now, if he went in for expensive sports equipment, things like that, it wouldn't be a problem, but Ray never spends a cent on himself. Have to save for the kids' college, he says. We never went ourselves." She almost smiled. "Shoot! I have to make him buy himself decent clothes for church.

"Your Aunt Caroline was one of the kindest people I ever met, and I know I'm going to miss her. She didn't charge me all that much, and I practiced over at the church. Still, all those lessons, and the music and all—well, they add up."

I nodded. I know what it's like on a budget. "That last day," I said. "Did she say or do anything different? I believe you might have been the last person to see her

53

alive."

Her small face turned as white as the magnolias in her hallway. "Oh, no. That couldn't be. My regular day's Monday, you know, and that week our daughter, Margo, had a dentist's appointment, so I had to cancel my lesson. I didn't see your aunt at all."

"Then why did Delia tell me she saw her there on Tuesday?" I said later to Augusta.

She didn't answer for a minute because she was learning a line dance—"The electric slide," she said—from a video she'd ordered using a "convenient toll-free number"—on *my* credit card of course, but Augusta always paid up. She had given up on aerobics—too exhausting, she said. And when I got home, I thought for a minute I'd wandered into the wrong apartment. Augusta flitted about my living room in an old dress of Aunt Caroline's, her hair tied back with a bright green ribbon. She fluttered her filmy skirt about her and sat on the wobbly footstool.

"Then one of them's not telling the truth," she said.

I nodded. "Bonita. Full of chickenshit if you ask me! Acts like she's afraid of something."

"Or somebody. And do you *have* to use that word?" Augusta shucked her gold sandals and wiggled bare pink toes. "Then I suppose we'll have to find out who or what it is."

I was about to ask her just how I was supposed to go about that when the telephone rang.

"Hi, hon," a familiar voice said. "Look, I guess I'm in the doghouse with you, but tell me it's not too late to make up. Please?"

Todd Burkholder! *Aaack*! I hung up the receiver and brushed my teeth three times. Just hearing his deceitful voice made me want to scour the room with industrial-strength antiseptic. How did he know how to find me?

After the second time he called I turned off the phone. The next day I brought my puppy home. I doubted if he'd bite, and he scared himself when he barked, but he could dam sure lick somebody to death!

# CHAPTER 7

THE WAILING KNIFED THROUGH WALLS, CRASHED OFF the ceiling, and scraped at my eardrums like fingernails on a chalkboard. Even the African violets in the window seemed to droop, curling furry leaves around their fragile faces.

" 'A-a-ma-a-zing gra-a-a-ce, how swe-e-e-t the sound, that saved a-ah wretch like me-e-e . . .' "

Miss Fronie was at it again, and it was amazing to me there was a window left unshattered in the house. After agonizing minutes of catlike screeching—warming up, she called it—my landlady plunged with gusto into her vocal repertoire, her volume tuned to torture.

Augusta huddled in Uncle Henry's old brown chair with a knitted cap pulled over her beautiful hair, a wad of socks stuffed underneath to cover each ear. "How much longer?" she asked. Her seagreen eyes betrayed any pretense at tranquillity. Fronie Temple had broken the angel barrier.

"It's good for your constitution," I said. As awful as the singing was, I couldn't deny a touch of satisfaction in this small, earthly dent in Augusta's heavenly glowcoat.

Hairy Brown sat at the angel's feet, ears perked, his large head following the sound. If dogs could smile, this one would be close to laughing. "I think he *likes* it," I said.

While the two of us cringed, Hairy kept time with his tail. And when, after a blessed pause, Fronie squawked forth with her version of "The Holy City," my tone-deaf puppy leaned forward on his haunches, lifted his shaggy head skyward, and joined in—not unlike people I've seen, who, filled with beer and camaraderie, gather around the piano to harmonize.

" 'Jer-u-sa-lemmm . . . ' " Fronie trilled. " 'Lift up your gates and s-i-i-n-g!' "

And Hairy Brown did. His loud, high-pitched howling made Augusta clutch her padded ears and shudder.

"Hush, Hairy!" I yelled, pulling his wiry brown head into my chest. "She'll hear you, be quiet." But it didn't do any good. Hairy gave an encore.

"You were going to have to ask her sometime," Augusta said with what I thought was a slight note of I-told-you-so in her voice. "We can't keep an animal this big out of sight forever." And she reached down to scratch behind a floppy ear, which made the dog lean against her knee and bay anew with pleasure.

I'll have to admit I was a little jealous. When Augusta was around, my puppy followed her about as though he thought she was his mother. Now he took time out to lick her hand.

"I guess you're right," I said, giving up on trying to muffle my musical hound. "Might as well get it over with."

Maybe she hadn't heard him, I thought as I plodded, head down, around to the front of the house where Fronie banged accompanying chords on the piano in her living room. She had moved on now to something that sounded vaguely like a hymn I used to sing in Sunday school, and if a song can be in pain, this one was screaming for mercy.

I saw his feet as I turned the corner, but it was too late. He held out a hand, stepped back to avoid me, but I was hell-bent on a collision. I smacked into him anyway.

"Oomph!" He was tall and good-looking. And I do mean good-looking. He stumbled, then steadied himself. "Sorry," the man said, though of course it wasn't his fault.

"Excuse me." I tried to edge around him. This must be the tenant who lived above me, the one with extremely heavy feet. He'd been out of town on a sales trip, my landlady said, and peace and quiet had reigned.

Until now. I didn't like the way he smiled at me—an invitation to start something. And I didn't care for the way dark hair curled at his temples, or for those adorable little crinkles around teasing blue eyes. Bah! I thought. Humbug!

Now he held out a hand. "If you're coming to complain, I warn you, it won't do a bit of good. The best we can do is pray for laryngitis."

A sense of humor, no less! And his teeth looked like a toothpaste commerical. I made a wimpy kind of noise and let him wrap my hand in his.

"You must be my downstairs neighbor. I'm Kent Coffey—glad I finally got to meet the lady who likes swing. Sometimes I hear it on your stereo."

Augusta, of course, and her Benny Goodman collection. I let this pass, still, he waited expectantly. Here's where I'm supposed to get all coy and silly, say something clever. Well, I had been through this before. Hadn't Todd the Bod been all smoothness and smiles?

Until he met his female counterpart in the Body Beautiful.

"Mary George Murphy." I extracted my hand and made myself turn away. It was hard not to look at him. My head came to his shoulder, I noticed as I walked past. Perfect for dancing—if I were interested in that sort of thing—which, of course, I wasn't. I wasn't a very good dancer, always felt clumsy somehow.

"Well, guess I'll be seeing you," he said after me.

"Sure," I said. But I didn't mean it.

Fronie Temple saw me through her window and motioned me inside. I sidled through the entrance hall with my hands at my sides, afraid I might break something. The room was filled with bric-a-brac, and little crocheted doilies like huge snowflakes covered every available surface—except for the piano. That was draped in a pink fringed shawl, and in the center, shattering roses wilted in a huge blue vase. The roses reminded me of my landlady, once bright and beautiful, now past their time. One advantage of looking rather ordinary, I thought, is that old age wouldn't be such a jolt.

A really awful painting of Fronie as a young woman hung over the mantel, flanked, I learned later, by pictures of her former husbands, the late Mr. Temple— "Tempie," she called him—whom I remembered vaguely, and the one before him, whom I didn't.

"Mary George! Come in, I hope my singing isn't a nuisance."

Nuisance wasn't the word I'd choose. "No, of course not! I'm afraid I'm the one who should apologize. I came about the dog."

"Dog?" She removed her bifocals to reveal faded blue eyes.

I sighed. "I have this puppy. . ." Oh, hell, Mary George, get on with it! "This very large puppy. You must have heard him 'singing?' "

"That was your dog? My goodness, I thought we were being stalked by the Hound of the Baskervilles! You didn't tell me you had a pet, Mary George."

I thought about the new paint job, the shiny kitchen floor. I couldn't blame her if she threw me out. But where would we go?

"I didn't have one," I explained. "Well, not until I started working for Doc Nichols at the animal clinic, and this dog was going to be destroyed. . . . Oh, Miss Fronie, he's such a sweetie! I just couldn't let anything happen to him. And then there were those break-ins."

*You are totally evil, Mary George Murphy! You haven't heard about any break-ins. But surely there must've been some around here*, I thought.

Fronie Temple held a plump hand to her heart. "What break-ins?"

"Petty things mostly. No place is immune to crime, Miss Fronie, not even Troublesome Creek." How many times had I heard Aunt Caroline say that? And she was right. But I didn't think the person who murdered my aunt was after valuables.

"We are kind of isolated here," I reminded her. "And living alone like this, I just feel safer with a dog around." Hairy Brown had barked twice in the few days I'd had him here—once at a cat on TV and again when he woke from a nap and caught sight of his tail.

Fronie looked at her hands, twisted a rather large ring on her finger. She was going to tell me to leave, I just knew it.

"He's very clean," I said. "And smart! I haven't had a bit of trouble training him. Usually I come home for lunch, so it's not a problem to take him out for a few minutes . . ."

She rubbed her arm, glanced out the window. "It's always been my policy—"

"I'm sorry," I said. "I should've asked. I'm sure Doc Nichols will board him while I look for another place."

"It's always been my policy . . . not to have a policy," Fronie Temple said finally. "Animals, as well as people, deserve to be considered on an individual basis. Now, when do I get to meet this mammoth puppy of yours?"

If I hadn't been afraid of smearing her makeup, I would've hugged her neck. Jamming my hands in my pockets so as not to break any doodads, I headed for the door. "Right now," I said. "Just follow me—and I promise you're going to love him!"

Hairy Brown gave my landlady the once-over, then wallowed shamelessly at her feet and allowed her to tickle his tummy.

"I suppose you've met our upstairs neighbor," Miss Fronie said, looking about. She seemed to approve of the room. I'd finally found a place for everything, except what was under my bed in a box.

"Briefly," I said. "Kind of reminds me of one of those glamorous movie actors from the fifties."

Fronie Temple smiled as she adjusted a dangling earring. "Looks a little like my first husband. But he seems quiet enough, minds his own business."

She paused at my kitchen door on her way out. "I like that ivy on the shelf by the window, Mary George. Nice touch. Did you ever find that jar you were looking for?"

"Not yet, but I'm not giving up." I had called several of the people I remembered being at the yard sale, but none of them had purchased the ceramic dog.

I followed her to the door. "Miss Fronie, did Aunt

60

Caroline ever mention a male visitor, one who came on a regular basis?"

"Oh, you are naughty, Mary George! Shame on you! You know your aunt wasn't like that." Fronie laughed as she gave me a playful pat.

"I don't mean like *that*. Delia said she'd seen somebody over there from time to time."

"Maybe Delia Sims was a little jealous," Fronie said in what I'm sure was meant to be a teasing voice. "You know there was a little conflict there."

"No, I didn't know," I said.

Fronie frowned. "Never did learn what it was. Tempie and I came here soon after we married, you know, and I've never heard anyone mention it, but there was a strain between those two."

*And there's a strain on your brain*, I thought as I closed the door behind her. My aunt and Delia Sims had been good friends as long as I could remember. If there had been a problem between them, Aunt Caroline would have told me. Wouldn't she?

With Hairy curled on the rug by my bed, I slept well that night for the first time since Aunt Caroline died. But each time the phone rang I had to force myself to answer, dreading to hear Todd Burkholder's voice on the other end of the line. To be honest, a secret part of me gloated at the delicious justice of rejecting him, but Todd's rekindled interest annoyed me and I didn't have the time or the patience to deal with it. Thank goodness he hadn't called again since that first night, and I hoped he had gotten the message. I almost put him out of my mind.

Until the next day.

We had a waiting room full of sick animals and a

61

terrified cat crying to get out of her carrier. Earlier, a boxer had escaped from his owner and cornered a whimpering Chihuahua behind the settee.

When the phone rang for the third time in five minutes, I tried not to sound impatient. "Animal clinic."

"Mary George? Don't you dare hang up on me. We're going to talk."

"No, we're not. Where did you get my number?"

"That woman who lived across from you. What's her name? Valerie. Said you'd moved back home and were working for a vet. Duh, Mary George, this was the only one in the phone book!"

I remembered chatting briefly with my neighbor when I went back to Charlotte to close my apartment and collect the rest of my belongings. Naturally it didn't occur to me that Todd the totally odd would come sniffing along behind me.

"I mean it, Todd. Don't call me here, or anywhere else, again!"

And he didn't—for a couple of hours at least. By the end of the afternoon we had worked our way to the last three patients—a cat with a kidney infection and two dogs waiting for microchip implants.

The electronic identification chip is a new method for keeping track of animals. It's about the size of a grain of rice and is inserted into the pet's skin with a large needle. I had Doc Nichols implant one in Hairy Brown before I took him home. Now if he ever gets lost and turns up at an animal shelter, the microchip will cause a scanner to beep and display his identification number. Unlike a dog tag, the chip is supposed to last a lifetime and can't fall off. At the clinic we've inserted one or two a day since the technique became available, and although it only takes a few minutes, it had been a busy day, and all of us were ready to go home.

I was reviewing the next day's appointments and wondering how we could possibly fit them all in when the telephone rang again. Oh, please! I thought. Don't let it be an emergency! Doc Nichols was just finishing the last implant.

"I'll see you after work," Todd said. "Your place. Be there."

"You're hallucinating, Todd. Have you been eating funny mushrooms?"

"I'm serious, Mary George. I made a big mistake when I broke off with you, but I won't make it again. I'm not letting you go."

"Excuse me," I said. "I think you'd better take a reality pill. Take a whole bottle of them!" And I slammed the receiver back in place. There was something in his voice that made me want to wrap myself in a blanket and hide.

About that time Doc came out of the examining room and threw his green smock into the laundry bin. He took one look at my face. "What's wrong, Sport? You're about the same color as the underside of a turnip green."

"It's nothing," I told him, and cried.

When I was composed enough to talk, I told him about Todd Burkholder and the phone calls, how he had dumped me for the aerobics instructor. "I'm being silly, I know, but I just can't handle this right now."

"If the damn fool calls again, you let me deal with him," Doc Nichols said with a fatherly pat on my shoulder. "I won't let him bother you here."

But what about when I wasn't here? As much as I loved my dog, I doubted if he'd be much protection. And I knew Todd had a nasty temper, although he'd

63

been careful not to show it until now. I had met Todd at a party at Missy Helms's who worked in my office building. Todd had dated a friend of hers, Missy said, until he became a little too possessive. She had tried to warn me, but I wouldn't listen. I guess I just didn't want to hear.

To get to the entrance of my apartment in the rear of Miss Fronie's, you had to wander through a maze of trees and shrubbery that screened the house from the street. Who would see or hear me if I yelled? I was honest-to-God afraid to go home.

And that was why I went weak-kneed with relief when I found Kent Coffey at my door with a long-stemmed red rose and an invitation to dinner.

# CHAPTER 8

"FRONIE SAYS YOU HAD A HOT DATE LAST NIGHT," Delia remarked the next day when I dropped by her place after work.

And that wasn't all Fronie said, I thought. I wanted to ask our old neighbor about her relationship with my aunt, but I couldn't think of a way to do it without being rude and intrusive.

I shrugged. "Miss Fronie talks too much. I did go out with the guy who lives upstairs, Kent Coffey. Went to that fish camp down by the river, but the only thing *hot* was the cocktail sauce."

Delia cuddled a huge orange tabby. "And?" she said, looking up at me.

"And nothing. He's very good-looking, seems nice. The shrimp was delicious, but the hush puppies had sugar in them. We got home before ten."

"Oh," she said. The tabby thumped to the floor and gave me a hateful cat glare.

"Actually, I had a very good time," I said, feeling a little guilty for being abrupt. I had been eager to go somewhere, anywhere away from my apartment, away from Todd Burkholder. But I didn't tell Delia that. "Kent's a manufacturer's rep," I explained. "Works for that new systems company just outside of town."

"Think you'll go out with him again?"

"I don't know. Maybe. He's good company, but I'm not ready for anything serious. Besides, I don't know much about him." I didn't want to repeat the mistake I'd made with Todd, but it gave my sagging ego a boost to know somebody desired my company. And of course it didn't hurt that he looked like a flesh-and-blood fantasy—mine, to be exact. But I had learned the hard way to watch my step.

Delia bent to stroke a purring calico. "You're right to take it slow. I certainly wouldn't rush into anything, but surely Fronie knows his background."

She seemed to have something on her mind. Did she know something I didn't?

"I don't think she knows any more than I do. He's quiet and minds his business, she says, and has been with her since January.

"Look, Kent's not the least bit sinister or anything. He's just a guy who wanted company for dinner. That's all." Delia was as bad as Aunt Caroline! Did she expect a résumé, complete with family history? I did wonder, though, why someone as handsome as my upstairs neighbor would choose to ask me out, especially when I'd been out-and-out rude when we met. Surely there were a lot of single women eager to date him.

We sat in sagging wicker chairs on my neighbor's

back porch with the whish-whish of the ceiling fan and the cloying smell of gardenias by the steps. Outside the cicadas tuned up for their summer evening serenade. "Well, I have good news and bad news," Delia said, refilling the iced tea in our glasses. "I think I know who bought your cookie jar."

"Great! When can I pick it up?"

"That's the bad news. There's a problem. I ran into Lottie Greenson in the post office this morning—knew I'd seen her at the yard sale with Edith Shugart. They go everywhere together—cousins, you know. Anyway, turns out Edith was the one who bought the china dog, only the Shugarts are on vacation. Aren't due back for several weeks."

"Isn't there any way to reach her? A phone number or something?"

"Not unless you want to try to chase her around Europe. They're on one of those tours. You know, dinner in Paris, lunch in Venice—that sort of thing."

"But when will they be back? Isn't there some way her cousin could get it for me?"

"Not without checking with Edith first. I'm afraid you'll just have to wait, Mary George," Delia said.

Still I wrote down the woman's name. Delia didn't think the Shugarts were due back anytime soon, but it wouldn't hurt to call.

Delia reached over and patted my arm. "We'll find it, honey. Don't worry. It isn't going anywhere."

She was right. It wouldn't help Aunt Caroline's cause to get all worked up over something I couldn't change. I took a long swallow of tea, sweet and cold, and closed my eyes, relishing the peace of the moment. At least that idiot Todd hadn't come calling the night before, or if he had he hadn't found me at home. And he hadn't phoned today either. Yet.

One of Delia's four cats—the gray striped one with a white-tipped tail—rubbed against my ankles, making me welcome in spite of my dog scent. I would miss this old house. "When do I get a tour of the condo?" I asked. "I thought you were going to put your house on the market."

Clink! Clink! Delia rattled ice in her glass, stared into the amber liquid like a fortune-teller searching for the future. "They won't take pets," she said, more to the cat at my feet than to me.

"Who won't?"

"Those people developing the condos. Pine Thicket Paradise, they call it. How can it be paradise if they won't let me bring my kitties? Mary George, what am I going do?"

"I can't imagine Delia Sims without a cat draped around her," I said to Augusta that night. "Why, she'd be miserable without her pets. I know how lonely I'd be without Hairy, even in the short time I've had him. I took forward every day to his being here when I come home." And I reached down to stroke the dog's head. He made one of his agreeable doggie grunts and pawed my knee.

Augusta sat in my aunt's rocking chair with a sewing basket on her lap. She was making a skirt for herself, a beautiful filmy skirt of gold and green and blue all melting into each other. It didn't even look like the same cloth I'd bought for her at Dorothy's Fabric Shop. "That's all very well and good," she said with a slight flutter. "But you're much too young to rely on a dog for company, Mary George."

"You can depend on dogs," I said. "Unlike some

people I know."

She raised her eyes toward the ceiling. "For heaven's sake, child, you've had *one* unfortunate romance . . ."

"Guess again," I said.

"Oh. Well, then, there's that young man upstairs. He certainly seems interested."

"Huh!" I said. "I doubt it. Desperate's more like it."

Augusta frowned. "Now, why would you say that? I don't like to encourage vanity, Mary George. Pretty is as pretty does, I've always said, but there's not a thing wrong with your looks. In fact, you remind me a bit of Shirley Sue Hawthorne."

"Shirley Sue Hawthorne? Who's that?" I tried to keep a straight face. I was still having a problem with the vanity bit.

"One of my temp assignments back in the thirties—just after talkies came out. An actress. Did very well in silent films, but talked like she had marbles up her nose."

"I thought all those early movie stars were tiny and blond." Augusta was only trying to boost my confidence. I couldn't imagine looking like a film star, silent or otherwise.

"Not Shirley Sue." Augusta shook out her skirt and examined it. It looked iridescent in the lamplight. "In fact, she might have been a little taller than you, and her eyes were brown as buckeyes. You have hair like hers too, except yours might have a bit more red in it." Augusta sat down and began to hem her skirt. The needle flashed in and out faster than any sewing machine. "There's not a thing wrong with your *looks*, Mary George Murphy!"

I smiled. Couldn't help it. Maybe she was making this up, but I didn't care. "What happened to her?" I asked. "Shirley Sue. Did she have to give up acting?"

"Naturally I had to guide her into another profession," Augusta said. "Fortunately Shirley Sue was tall and willowy, fantastic dancer, and that was just before they started making all those grand musicals. She didn't want for work. And later, I believe, she opened her own studio."

Augusta swirled the skirt over her head and fastened it at the waist. "Fact is, she was the one who taught me to dance," she said, twirling into the bedroom and out— with just a light pause in front of the mirror.

"Good thing you didn't have to wait to learn from me," I said, and found myself being pulled to my feet and whisked to the middle of the floor while Augusta punched a tape into the VCR. She detested daytime television—it embarrassed her, she said—all those intimate commercials, and people doing and saying things to make even a statue blush, although sometimes I'd hear her late at night laughing at *I Love Lucy* reruns. But she loved the VCR, and I kept her supplied with rented tapes of the good old forties stuff. In fact, I was becoming addicted myself.

Now, with Augusta at my side and "Achy Breaky Heart" coming at me from the TV screen, I was being forced to do confusing, bouncy things with my feet in time to the music.

"Don't look down!" Augusta commanded, jabbing me in the ribs with a sling of her wrist. "Watch the screen, watch me. You'll get the hang of it."

We went through the steps six times, and just when I thought I'd get to rest, she fast-forwarded into a fiendish stomper called "The Boot-Scootin' Boogie."

I slept like a zombie that night. And when Kent called

the next day and invited me out for Saturday night, I secretly hoped we'd go dancing.

We went to a movie instead—Dutch, because Kent was a little short on cash, but that was okay—and stopped afterward for ice cream at the Hound Dog Café.

Kent kissed me good night at the door, but I didn't ask him in, although I think he expected me to. Frankly, I wasn't in the mood for anything more. Not with Kent, not with anybody. Not yet.

What was the matter with me? Was it because of what happened with Todd? Although any positive feelings I'd had for the man were zilch, and I felt I owed a thank-you note to his little aerobics bimbo. After a couple of days of comparative peace, he'd called me twice at home and once at the clinic, until finally I'd threatened him with the police. My taste of sweet revenge had turned to vinegar, and I just wanted this creep to leave me alone.

Now I lay in bed listening to night noises outside my window. Hairy Brown snoozed on the floor beside me, and Augusta had taken off to wherever she goes when she's not around. A squirrel scuttled over the roof, and branches brushed the side of the old house. At least I hoped it was branches.

Could Todd Burkholder have had anything to do with what happened to Aunt Caroline? But that didn't add up. On the day my aunt died, Todd was still making out hot and heavy with that woman next door. Wasn't he? Yet Delia had mentioned seeing a strange man across the street, someone my aunt hadn't wanted to discuss.

I had an awful thought that Aunt Caroline might have bribed Todd to break off with me, but bribed him with what? And what was Bonita Moody trying to hide? She had denied being at Aunt Caroline's the day my aunt

70

died, even though Delia swears she saw her there. Unless Delia herself wasn't telling the truth . . . but I didn't want to think about that.

The only thing I was certain of was that whoever was responsible for my aunt's death was looking for my family Bible, and for all I knew, they had already found it. Unless Aunt Caroline hid it where none of us would ever think to look.

Suddenly the room seemed close and dark. And quiet. I seemed to exist in a black void. Alone. I had felt this way when I was five and my parents died in that horrible wreck, until Sam made the ultimate gesture and let me keep his turtle overnight. From then on, he made every day an adventure: stringing a vine bridge over the creek (we both fell in), following the tracks of the wild and terrible "clopadopalous" that turned out to be a neighbor's mule. I smiled, remembering how we'd collected lightning bugs and turned them loose in Cookie's room while she slept. Cindy, the young apprentice cook, was generous and noted for her sticky buns, but hateful Cookie was not only stingy with her portions but a tattletale as well.

I remembered Sam's face at ten, sunburned and smiling, his eyes sparkling with exciting news he just couldn't wait to tell. What would he be like now? And why would I even care? But I did. Lately he had been more and more on my mind.

"Night is just day painted over," I thought just before sleep. I wanted my old friend back. Maybe I'd never find him; or worse, I might be sorry if I did. But I knew I had to try. I had to find my Sam.

# CHAPTER 9

"CHILDREN'S HOME? NO, I DON'T KNOW OF ANY children's home around here." The waitress poised, pad in hand, and totaled my breakfast bill. She looked to be around forty-plus, certainly old enough to remember. And a place that big couldn't just disappear.

The woman refilled my coffee cup without my even asking and whisked away the empty plate. The doc had closed the clinic for the day because of his niece's wedding and I'd taken advantage of my time off to drive almost eighty miles to the little foothill town of Hughes, North Carolina, where Summerwood was located. Now, having treated myself to sausage and biscuits, along with grits and red-eye gravy, at a tiny diner that was once a railroad car, I felt I'd driven into the Twilight Zone.

"Summerwood Acres," I said. "It's only a few miles outside of town." What little spending money we'd had never made it farther than here. Hughes was synonymous to me with movies and ice cream cones. How could anyone overlook more than a hundred children?

"I've only been here a couple of years," the waitress said, obviously noticing my disappointment. "Why don't you ask Gail? She's lived around here forever."

I thanked her and left a tip, then stood in line to pay my bill and speak with the cashier who'd been pointed out to me.

Gail was a small, perky woman with bright brown eyes and a quick smile. "Oh, honey, are you one of the Summerwood kids?" she asked when I repeated my question, and I knew by the way she said it that something had gone wrong.

"I was for a while, but that was a long time ago. I just thought I'd look up some people I knew there." I hadn't been back to Summerwood Acres since I went to live with Aunt Caroline and Uncle Henry. My aunt was afraid it would upset me, remind me of my parents' death, and with Sam gone, I had no good reason to visit.

"Oh, my goodness," Gail said, and she didn't look as vivacious anymore. "I guess you haven't been here in a while. The children's home burned—or most of it did—about three or four years ago. Lightning, they say. Happened during a storm. Thank goodness no one was hurt!"

I thought of all those records. "Was anything left?"

She gave me my change and shoved the cash drawer shut. "Not much, I'm afraid. The main hall burned to the ground, but they saved the kitchen wing and one of the dorms—I think it was the boys'. A while back somebody tried to turn the place into some kind of camp, but I reckon it must've fizzled. Haven't heard any more about it."

"What happened to the people who worked there?" I'd never find Sam now, or anybody who knew him.

She shook her head. "Oh, Lord, who knows! I expect some of them retired." Then suddenly she smiled. "Hey, I'll bet Ambrose would know! Ambrose Dunn. Remember him? Used to be caretaker there. Married to a cousin of mine, and hasn't worked a lick since the fire."

I didn't remember Ambrose, I said, but I'd sure like to meet him.

"Then you won't have far to go." Gail led me to the window. "See that row of men on the bench in front of the hardware store? The second from the left is Ambrose. They've helped to solve the world's problems three times over without ever leaving that bench. I'm sure you must've noticed a difference," she added, laughing.

"I'll try and remember to thank them, " I told her as I left.

Ambrose wore a neatly ironed short-sleeved dress shirt, Bermuda shorts—faded blue and baggy—and black calf-length socks with an expanse of skinny white leg in between. He looked like the type who might consider whittling if it weren't too strenuous. But he was polite and offered me a seat.

"Thank you, no. Please don't get up," I said, as if there were any real danger of this. "I'm trying to find anyone who might have worked at the children's home at Summerwood twenty years ago or more. I understand there was a fire."

He nodded sadly. "Happened on a Sunday when 'most everybody was at church. A miracle nobody was hurt." The other four men inclined their heads in solemn agreement.

I stood surrounded by silence. Ambrose didn't do anything quickly, I supposed. "You might try Bernice Butler, used to be matron in the boys' building," he said finally. "Somebody told me she's working at that big department store over in High Point—or she was."

I smiled. I remembered Mrs. Butler. Sam had called her Miss Pooh because she reminded him of the bear in the story. Ambrose looked as though he'd drifted off to sleep, and I resisted the urge to shake him. "What department store?" I asked. "Belk? Dillard's?" I started to run through my list.

"That's right, one of them. Or it could've been

Sears." He squinted at the sun, then glanced at his pocket watch, to see, I guess, if one of them was wrong. "Can't remember which." Ambrose Dunn was done.

"Oh, good! You've brought coffee." Augusta waited in my car parked under the redbud tree in front of the Methodist church. "And my sausage biscuit?"

I handed over the paper-wrapped sandwich, thinking of all the calories I'd consumed. But with Augusta and Hairy to keep me company, I had started walking several miles at dusk almost every night, so maybe it wouldn't all go to my hips.

Augusta took a bite of the biscuit and washed it down with coffee. She looked as if she might be in the midst of some kind of religious experience. I knew better than to interrupt. When the sausage biscuit was gone, she cleaned each finger with dainty little kitten kisses, arranged her chiffonlike skirt about her, and raised a brow. "Well, what did you find out?"

I told her. "Looks like we'll have to drive to High Point, but it's only about thirty miles from here."

"I know that," Augusta said, sipping primly from her cup.

"But first I'd like to take a look at the home, or what's left of it," I said. "It's on the way . . . but then I guess you knew that too."

The arch over the entrance, flanked by huge red oaks, still read Summerwood Acres, but at the end of the curving drive I saw nothing but weeds where the main hall used to be. Someone had evidently attempted to landscape the grounds around the kitchen and dining area with a border of petunias and what appeared to be a grape arbor. Several benches waited in its shade.

"Look, somebody's planted a garden," Augusta pointed out as I pulled timidly under the arch and stopped. A red pickup was parked in the shade of the building that used to house the boys, and behind it a man and several children picked something, probably beans.

I turned around quickly and headed out. "Looks like they've rented the land," I said, glad that someone was using the property.

"Is there another way to High Point?" Augusta asked after a few minutes.

"A road runs parallel to this, but it winds around a lot. Might take longer that way. Why?"

"I think somebody's following us," she said, frowning over her shoulder. "Kind of a dingy gray car, see it coming around the curve there? It passed us when we turned into the drive back at Summerwood, but they must have parked somewhere and waited, because here it is behind us again."

"Maybe they had to stop, check a map or something. Doesn't mean they're following us." I glanced in the rearview mirror. Todd Burkholder had an old gray Mustang he loved almost as much as he loved himself. I stepped on the accelerator, but the other car maintained its distance behind me, lagging just far enough behind so I couldn't get a good look. "Uh-oh," I said. "Give me a break!" This was no place to meet up with an irrational ex-boyfriend.

According to the road map, we should be close to the turn-off to the connecting road to the other route, and about a mile later, I slowed just enough to make a right turn. Luckily a small convenience store, surrounded by cars, was just around the corner. I circled behind it and waited. Sure enough, here came the dusty gray car. It slowed just a little as it passed the store—to see if I was there, I guess—then drove on.

"A-ha!" Augusta said. "Didn't I tell you? Could you see who it was?"

"Too far away. Might've been a Mustang, but I couldn't tell from here." Surely that fool Todd had gotten the message by now. I waited until the car disappeared over a hill, then scooted out the way we had come. The gray car might still overtake us, but it would require some swift maneuvering.

"Mustang? I thought that was a horse." Augusta leaned out the window to watch behind us. "Can't you go any faster, Mary George?" Her bright hair swirled about her, a tangle of silken firelight, and when she laughed I forgot about being afraid. Suddenly I started to giggle. I hadn't felt like this since Sam and I stole Cookie's double-D bra off the clothesline and put it on our "snow lady."

I had dreamed again of Sam the night before—only this time he looked older, and he sat on the steps of the main building at Summerwood with my aunt's cookie jar in his lap and a letter in his hand. Yet no matter how hard I tried, I couldn't read what was written there.

When we drove into High Point a short while later, I had a feeling I was that much closer to finding him.

We started with the largest mall we could find. Bernice Butler, I was told, worked in the lingerie department at Belk, and while Augusta disappeared among the frothy undies, I selected a short summer gown and stood in line to wait. In spite of her graying hair, the former matron still resembled the bear of storybook fame, and when she looked up at me with her questioning brown eyes and rather large nose, I smiled wider than usual.

"I remember you from Summerwood," I told her, introducing myself. "And I'm hoping you can help me locate a boy I used to know there . . . He'd be a man now, of course. His name is Sam. I don't think I ever knew his last name."

Bernice grabbed my hand in both of hers and hung on for dear life. "My goodness . . . so you're one of ours! Oh, I do miss that old place! Do you live around here?"

I told her I didn't and reminded her about Sam as she finally got around to ringing up the gown.

"Sam? Goodness, I don't remember anyone named Sam. Of course that was almost twenty years ago. But even if I did, I probably wouldn't know where to find him. Some of my boys kept in touch for a while— mostly the older ones, but after the fire I'm afraid I lost track."

She wore a mustard-colored dress with a white collar and had sort of a Pooh Bear shape. Now she rested her hands on her stomach. "Why don't you try Mr. Mac? You remember him, don't you? Lives in a retirement center this side of Charlotte. Might want to call before you go, though. He does a lot of volunteering over there."

I did remember Mr. Mac, the minister who headed the children's home, and was always a little in awe of him, although I had no reason to be. The Reverend Edwin J. McCallister was a quiet, preoccupied man who ate with us in the dining hall and called us each by name. Surely he would remember Sam.

While Augusta checked out the fast-food offerings, I phoned Mr. Mac at Carolina Towers from the concessions area of the mall. He was just getting ready to leave for a session with his literacy student he said, but would be glad to help if he could.

78

I told him about Sam. "Miss P—Mrs. Butler doesn't remember him," I said. "And I don't even know his last name. Do you have any idea what happened to him? He would have been about ten or eleven when he left there eighteen years ago."

"Goodness, that's been a while. Sam. Sounds familiar, but I can't place him, and of course you know our records were destroyed."

"He had brown hair that wouldn't stay down if you glued it . . . and freckles, I think. I'm almost sure about the freckles. His eyes were sort of a greenish gray . . . and he liked turtles."

Mr. Mac laughed. "That description would fit several of our boys, but I think I know which one you mean. I just can't come up with a name. Sam was a nickname, I believe. Do you remember him being called by anything other than that?"

"Just Sam, I said.

"And you say he was several years older than you?"

"Three," I said. "He was in the fifth grade when he left."

"Well, there you are," the reverend said. "The elementary school over in Hughes would have those records. In fact, I believe Geraldine Thompson's still on the faculty there. She's taught fifth grade about as long as I can remember. I'll give her a call if you'd like, see if she has time to see you."

"That would be great," I said. Now, why didn't I think of that?

I stood guard by the pay phone pretending to look up a number until the minister called back. Mrs. Thompson would be glad to speak with me, he said. She was just finishing with her early session of summer school, and if I could get there by three, I'd find her still there. "You

79

do remember where the school is?" Mr. Mac asked.

That was one thing I wasn't likely to forget, I assured him.

"It's a shame that camp thing didn't work out," he said. "They lost their funding from the church, and I'm afraid they'll have to close."

"What happened?"

"Several people wanted to run Summerwood as a year-round camp for disadvantaged children. They depended on private funding, but just couldn't seem to get the support they needed. Right now I think they have a skeleton summer staff with less than twenty campers. Wish it could've worked out for them."

"That must have been some of the campers we saw in the garden back at Summerwood," I said to Augusta as we drove back the way we had come.

She mumbled happily and started on another wedge of pizza—a first for her. I'd introduced her to tacos the week before. "Rooshrwreenabnfahlud," she said, glancing in the mirror beside her.

"*What?*"

"I *said,* are you sure we're not being followed? That old gray car's not still behind us, is it?" Augusta patted her dainty mouth with a paper napkin.

I looked over my shoulder but didn't see anything there. In my excitement at meeting Sam's teacher I'd completely forgotten about the car that had trailed us earlier. Anyway, it was probably just a coincidence.

# CHAPTER 10

MRS. THOMPSON'S HAIR WAS THE SAME COLOR IT HAD been twenty years ago—Mercurochrome orange. And her classroom was still the second door on the left down the long, tiled hall. In spite of a bright new coat of yellow paint, the school smelled as it always did of chalk, musty raincoats, and the stuff they use to mop the floor, but the old place had shrunk. Still, I experienced a smattering of eight-year-old jitters in my twenty-six-year-old stomach as I waited to be recognized. The children condemned to summer school had gone home for the day, and Hughes Elementary, home of the Battling Baby Bruins, echoed every little sound.

"I'm sorry, I didn't hear you come in. It's Mary George, isn't it? Mr. Mac called about you." Geraldine Thompson smiled at me as she gathered a sheaf of lined papers and anchored them with a brightly painted rock. "Please sit down, and excuse the dust. If I saved what they brought in on their shoes from the playground, I could sell real estate."

I laughed. This was the same teacher who caught me running in the hall and made me walk the length of it six times. But now we were equals. Sort of.

"Tell me about yourself. Don't sit there—sun's in my face. I want to be able to see you. Mr. Mac says you were a Summerwood child. When were you in school here?"

I cleared my throat. "I only went to Hughes for three years—kindergarten through second grade. Mrs. Thompson, I came to ask you about—"

"And who was your teacher then?"

"In the second grade? Miss Lewis. Her name was

81

Miss Lewis." I loved my second grade teacher. She was young and pretty and let us make papier-mâché puppets.

"Ah, yes." Mrs. Thompson removed her glasses. "She married soon after that, I think. Moved away." She squinted at the glasses and then at me. "And after that?"

"Well, I would've had Mrs. Goldman, but I went to live in Troublesome Creek with—"

Geraldine Thompson jammed on her glasses and nodded. She'd heard enough about me. "Mr. Mac tells me you're looking for a friend of yours, someone you knew back at Summerwood."

I smiled. It occurred to me I was being tested. This teacher wasn't about to give information on one of her students to just any old riffraff off the street. Behind her, neatly written essays stapled to bright construction paper lined the bulletin board; laminated pictures of every American president marched along the wall. Mrs. Thompson meant business. Or, to use an expression of my aunt's, "She seen her duty and she done it!"

"Yes, ma'am," I said. "His name was Sam, and he would've been in your class when he left. It happened all of a sudden: one day he was here, and then he wasn't."

I remembered Sam telling me good-bye. He wasn't in his usual place at supper, and I wondered if he was sick. We had spaghetti that night and I was trying to see how big a wad I could twist around my fork when he slid into his chair beside me.

"Stop playing with your food and listen," he said. "And promise you won't cry. My dad's come for me and I've gotta go, but I'll write. . . . Listen, Mary George, I won't forget you. Look, I'm gonna let you keep my good-luck rock—see, it looks just like a frog. You can have it, Mary G—aw, darn it, now, don't cry!"

And now, years later, to my surprise and disgust, I felt the tears begin. "But he never wrote," I said. "I guess he forgot all about me." Oh Lord, what a silly thing to do! This woman would think I was a complete fool.

A box of tissues appeared under my nose and a worn old hand patted my arm. "He didn't forget you," Geraldine Thompson said.

"How do you know?" Under her watchful eye, I blew my nose and took another tissue.

"Because I happen to know your Sam, and if he didn't get in touch, he must've had a good reason." Her blue eyes sparkled with humor. Was this woman teasing me?

"Do you know where Sam is? Will you help me find him?" I had to sit on my hands to keep from vaulting over the desk. "Are you sure it's the same one?"

She stood and adjusted a window blind, inspected a cactus plant on the shelf below. "In the first place, Sam's only a nickname, a combination of initials. But then, I imagine you knew that."

"Not until Mr. Mac mentioned it. We always just called him Sam." Was I going to be denied because I didn't have the correct information? I had an awful feeling I'd failed the exam. "We were sort of like a family then; I guess last names weren't important." *Oh, please tell me where he is*! I would beg if I had to.

"If you'd come by this morning, you'd have found him right down the road. Sam volunteers his time several mornings a week at Camp Summerwood." She looked at the clock. "I expect he's left by now, but we can call if you like."

Now that I knew where I could find him, a spell of shyness came over me. What if Sam didn't want to see me? What if he'd changed? I took a couple of steps backward. "That's all right . . . don't want to trouble you. I'll try to get in touch tomorrow if you'll just give me a number where I can reach him."

But Mrs. Thompson wasn't letting me off the hook that easily. With a hand at my elbow, she propelled me out the door and down the hall. "Nonsense. No trouble at all! We can use the phone in the office. Maybe we'll catch him if we hurry!"

And hurry we did, but Sam, we were told, had left for the day. His former teacher seemed as disappointed as I was relieved. What was the matter with me?

For future reference, Mrs. Thompson told me, Sam's full name was Solomon Abel Maguire, and he left her class in March of his fifth grade year to live with his father who was in the military.

"As I understand it, when the boy's mother died, his father just wasn't financially or emotionally prepared to assume full-time care," the teacher said. "But as soon as he felt he could look after Sam, his dad came back for him."

She walked me to the door of the school where years before we'd lined up to wait for the bright yellow bus. The children from Summerwood always sat together.

"I knew several days before Sam did that his father was coming for him, but I was told not to say anything." Geraldine Thompson gave me a slip of paper with my old friend's name and address. "As happy as I was for Sam, I hated to lose him. Such curiosity! And he was never, never bored." She sighed. "You can't say that about many."

"Where did he go? Did you hear from him after he left?"

"Somewhere out West—California, I think. His dad

had arranged for a housekeeper to help look after him. And no, I didn't see or hear from Sam again until a couple of years ago. Came by here right after Summerwood burned. Of course I had no idea who he was at first." Mrs. Thompson smiled. "He's a teacher himself now. Junior high over near Salisbury. Biology."

"That figures," I said, and told her about the turtle named Imogene, the lightning-bug stunt. "I wonder if that's who we—I—saw in the garden at Summerwood this morning."

"Wouldn't be surprised. He's over there a good bit, and I doubt if they pay him a cent." She shook her head. "Good idea, that camp. I've helped out over there a few times myself, but it's going to take more than the little trickle they've got coming in to keep it going. Too many Indians, and not enough chiefs—if you know what I mean."

Augusta sat on a bench in the shade of a sycamore with her face toward the road and didn't look up as I approached.

"I've found him!" I said, but not loud enough for Mrs. Thompson to hear. I'm sure she already thought I was peculiar. I turned to wave good-bye to her, but the teacher's Raggedy Ann hair was already disappearing down the long hallway.

Still Augusta didn't budge.

"What are you doing?" I said. "Didn't you hear me? She told me where to find Sam."

I turned my back on her and walked to the car, leaving the driver's door open as I started the engine to give the air conditioning a chance to do its thing. The next thing I knew she was sitting beside me. "Sorry." Augusta said. "Guess I wasn't listening. I was watching

85

for our friend in the gray car with the funny name."

"What? Damn! Is he following us again?" I slammed and locked my car door. "When did you see him?"

"Not since we lost him back at that little country store this morning, but I don't think we've seen the last of him." Augusta did something with her hair, and in about two seconds, arranged it in sort of a pouf on top of her head. If she used any pins, I didn't see them. "And it really isn't necessary to use profanity, Mary George. There are other ways to express yourself."

I glared at her as we drove out of the parking lot and began the long drive home. It was the middle of June and at least ninety degrees, yet she looked as if she'd stepped out of one of those meadow-flower commercials for underarm deodorant. "Don't you ever get hot?" I said. How dare she sit there all cool and collected without even a "dew drop," as Aunt Caroline called it, on her forehead. "Why is it you never seem rumpled or sticky? Don't you ever sweat?"

Even her smile was refreshing. "I'm sorry if it annoys you, Mary George, but angels don't wilt."

"I didn't say 'wilt.'" I shoved a clump of hair from my face with a moist palm.

"Very well. We don't sweat," she said, and I felt her penetrating green-eyed gaze. "If you'd like, Mary George, when we get home, I believe I can do something with your hair."

"Just leave my hair out of it!" I took a curve a little faster than I should've and gritted my teeth when the tires squealed.

"Reckless driving isn't going to get you anywhere unless you're in a hurry to join your parents," my pious passenger reminded me. "If you're upset about something, I do wish you'd tell me about it. I should think you'd be happy about finding your friend." She glanced in the rearview mirror—to see, I guess, if we were being chased by the police. "You did say you knew where he was? Is that where you're going in such a rush?"

I didn't answer. It wasn't Augusta's fault I was afraid of meeting Sam, and I knew she only meant to help. But it can really be a pain in the ass having somebody around who is always right.

Augusta must've guessed my thoughts because suddenly she just wasn't there.

"Look, I'm sorry I hurt your feelings," I said. "You can come on back if you want." I waved my arm in the space where she'd been, and if anyone had seen me, they'd think I had lost my wits completely. Maybe they'd be right. "I know you're here somewhere, Augusta Goodnight. You might as well make yourself known."

She didn't reappear, but suddenly the radio came on, and when I heard the music, I had to laugh. The vocalist was singing "Fools Rush in Where Angels Fear to Tread."

I was still smiling when I turned into the rutted gravel drive to my apartment. My stomach reminded me it was after six o'clock. I hurried inside to let out the dog. Robbie, the little boy who lived behind us, had promised to take Hairy out at noon, but I knew the puppy would be scratching at the door after being cooped up.

But Hairy Brown wasn't there. I knew he wasn't there before I opened the door because he usually whimpers as soon as he hears my key, then throws himself upon me as I step inside.

"Hairy?" I stood in the living room and called his

name, hoping he'd come bounding out of the kitchen or the bedroom with his usual ecstatic doggy face. Where else could he be? I made myself check the other rooms, dreading what I might find, but the puppy wasn't there. The dog's bowl was half filled with food and the sack of puppy chow sat on the kitchen counter where Robbie had left it.

I clapped my hands, feeling a cast-iron weight plunge to the pit of my stomach. "Here, Hairy! Come on, boy!" But I knew I was wasting my time. Maybe Robbie had taken the dog home with him, or Hairy had gotten away from him. But the leash hung in its customary place by the kitchen door.

I was on my way to telephone when I noticed the books on my coffee table weren't exactly as I'd left them; the drawer to the end table sagged partially open. And there, behind my uncle's ugly old leather chair, the little needlepoint footstool with the wobbly leg lay on its side. Someone had ripped off the backing and torn away the trim. Whoever had been here was looking for something, and I didn't think they had found it.

But they would be back.

# CHAPTER 11

"BUT HAIRY WAS THERE WHEN I LEFT!" ROBBIE SAID. "I let him out just like you told me, and we played fetch for a while, then I fed him."

The boy had been practicing shots at a basketball hoop above the family's garage, and sweat trickled down his red face as he bounced the ball on the asphalt. "Hairy—he minds me real good. I wouldn't let him get away."

"I know that, Robbie. You take good care of him. But think about it—did you remember to lock the door?" I tried not to sound accusing, but somebody had ransacked my apartment, and it didn't look as if the lock had been forced.

He shrugged. "Twisted that knob thing the way you showed me—tried it too. That door was locked sure as I'm standing here." The ball bounced feebly, then rolled away into the grass. "I don't know how he got out."

"I believe you, Robbie, but I had to ask. You understand, don't you?" I paid him the three dollars we had agreed on, plus whatever change I had, and he stuffed it into his pocket. He didn't answer me, didn't look up.

"If you see Hairy, you'll let me know, won't you?"

He nodded, still not meeting my eyes. I wasn't forgiven yet.

"Old Hairy, he'll come if you call him I reckon. Always does," Robbie said.

But I had called until my throat hurt. I called some more.

The police, when I phoned, weren't unduly concerned about a missing pet.

"Ma'am, are you sure you had the door shut good? Dogs can be right smart, you know. Why, I've heard of—"

"Look, somebody searched my apartment," I said. "They were looking for something."

"Anything missing?" Did I detect a smidgen of interest in his voice?

"I told you—my dog—and who knows what else!"

"Somebody will be right over. That address again?"

I sat down to wait.

It didn't take long. The young policeman who showed up at my door looked familiar, so familiar I guess I must have stared.

"Dennis Henderson," I said finally.

He gave me a puzzled look.

"Miss Arnold's social studies. Eighth grade."

"Oh . . . yeah . . . right." I could tell he didn't remember me.

"Didn't you sing in the choir for a while? Aunt Caroline used to brag on your tenor."

Now he smiled. "Right! She's the one got me to liking music. In fact, I'm taking voice training now. Sure hated to hear about her accident. Your aunt was some nice lady!" He stood in the living room looking about as if he expected a guided tour.

I gave him one. "Look at this footstool—ripped apart! And that end table—somebody's been going through it. They've been in the bedroom too. Dresser drawers aren't quite right."

He frowned. "Aren't quite right?"

"Not like I left them. Everything's out of place. Now, about my dog. Have you heard anything?"

"Not yet. Anything else missing?"

"Not that I've noticed. Look, Hairy's still a puppy. I'm afraid he'd never find his way home, and he could get run over out there." I looked out the window as I spoke, hoping to glimpse his silly old shaggy head.

"Any idea who might've done this, or why?" He squatted to examine the remains of Aunt Caroline's needlepoint stool.

I shook my head. How could I explain about the missing Bible when I didn't even understand it myself?

"Notice anybody hanging around who doesn't belong?"

*Todd Burkholder.* I told him about being followed that morning and he scribbled something on a pad.

"See him after that?" he asked.

I shook my head. "Haven't seen him, or whoever it was, since we—I—lost him this side of High Point."

"You said *whoever it was*, so you're not sure it was this guy, Todd Burkholder, you saw?" Dennis hesitated, pen above pad. "What would he be looking for here? Anything in particular?"

I didn't know, unless it was me—which made me feel like my middle had turned to mush. I took a couple of deep breaths to keep from being sick.

"Any idea how he got in?" He inspected the door again, ran his hands along the windows. "Everything looks okay here. Who else has a key?"

"Miss Fronie, of course. And Robbie, the neighbor boy who fed the dog, but he returned it this afternoon." I found the key in my pocket and held it out for him to see. "I can't think of any reason why Robbie would tear the stool apart."

Dennis Henderson shook his head and grinned. "Miss Fronie? She that lady who sings in the choir?"

"Right. Fronie Temple's my landlady—owns this house." I shrugged. "If she wanted to search my apartment she could do it anytime while I was at work. Besides, Miss Fronie's been away all day. Had a dental appointment in Charlotte." I looked at my watch. "Should be back by now . . ." It was beginning to get dark. It wasn't like Fronie Temple to be out this late.

"Anyone else?" Dennis clicked his pen.

"Nobody else has a key, at least no one I can think of . . . unless . . ."

"What? Unless what?" Click. Click. Click. Click. The man was getting impatient.

91

"I almost forgot. I keep an extra key hidden outside in case I lose mine." I tend to be forgetful.

He actually rolled his eyes. "Don't tell me. Under the doormat?"

"Certainly not! It's under that loose brick on the top step—or was." The two of us hurried out to see if the key was still there. It was.

"Anybody know where you hide this?" Dennis asked.

"Not that I know of," I said.

He picked up the key, weighed it in his hands before giving it to me. "Not exactly the best hiding place; or somebody might've watched you put it there. I don't think I need to tell you not to do this again." Dennis shoved the brick back in place with his toe. There was a question in his eyes.

Todd Burkholder. It came back to him every time.

"What in the world's going on here? There's a police car in the drive!" Miss Fronie's lemony curls bobbed as she glanced about, taking in the carcass of the footstool, the young policeman trying his best to look in charge.

"Dennis Henderson! That you? What are you doing here? Mary George, what happened? Are you all right?"

"I'm fine, Miss Fronie," I said, enduring a couple of pats and a squeeze on the arm. "But there's been a break-in and Hairy Brown's gotten away, or else somebody's taken him."

To give her credit, I think she really tried to look sorry, but it just didn't work. "Oh, dear. Now, that's too bad. But why do you suppose anyone would . . . I mean, who would do a thing like that?"

"We're not sure," I said. "But it looks like they were searching for something."

"We'll do some checking on this Burkholder guy,"

Dennis said, stuffing his notebook in an inside pocket. "If he was here, we'll find out about it. Maybe we'll get lucky."

"But what about my dog? What about Hairy?"

"I'll ask around, but you might check with Animal Control. Of course if we hear anything, we'll let you know."

"And Todd? When will—"

"Doesn't look like he actually took anything, but you've given me his home address and we know where he works, so we should know something tomorrow."

"And then what?" I asked.

"It all depends," he said.

I waited until noon the next day to give Dennis Henderson a call.

"Meant to get back to you on that, Mary George," he said. "Afraid we've hit a dead end on the Burkholder angle. Claims he was making sales calls over in Burlington all morning and got back to the office around three. Secretary there backs him up. We'll be checking out the customers he says he called on over there, of course. See if he's telling the truth."

I didn't believe Todd Burkholder knew the truth from a toad on a log. If he left work even a few minutes early, he'd still have time to rip apart Aunt Caroline's footstool and poke about where he didn't belong. And now my dog was missing, the only living thing I had left to love.

I knew Todd had a rotten streak, but why would he want to do this to me? Was it because I didn't welcome him back like a silly, love-blind doormat after his erotic aerobic interlude? And hadn't he said I would be sorry?

Revenge. Pure and simple. Well, simple maybe, not pure. Anger rumbled deep inside me. My insides burned with the acid of resentment. He wasn't going to get away with this.

I snatched up the phone and called directory assistance.

"Mary George, honey! Well, this is a surprise! Finally had to admit you couldn't live without me, huh?"

That snake Todd not only had the nerve to pretend surprise at hearing from me, but he sounded almost convincing. Not enough.

"How dare you follow me yesterday, you slimy creep! I can't believe you had the nerve to slither around in my apartment while I was gone. This is absolutely the last straw! Did you really think I wouldn't suspect it was you?" I deliberately lowered my voice, glancing behind me to see if the doc had left for lunch. Good. His smock hung just inside the office door and his keys were missing from their usual place on his desk.

"What?" He laughed. It was that weak, sickening kind of laugh losers give when they know they're cornered. "Mary George, sugar, I do believe you've flipped out."

"Don't you call me sugar!" I wanted to gag at the sound of his voice. "Did you have to tear the place apart? Aunt Caroline's mother stitched that little footstool. What were you looking for, Todd?"

"Would you mind letting me in on your little game? Just what in hell are you talking about? I'll swear I haven't a clue." His voice was cool, remote.

"Don't pretend with me, Todd Burkholder. I've already talked with the police. What have you done with my dog? If anything's happened to Hairy, I'll make hell seem like a winter resort!"

"So that's what all those questions were about. Some guy was over here this morning annoying the secretary,

94

making a nuisance of himself. Thought maybe a car like mine had been involved in an accident—or a robbery—something like that. Just what is it I'm supposed to have done?"

I told him. "I saw you, Todd. Out past Hughes near that intersection. And then when I got home, somebody had searched my apartment and Hairy Brown was gone. I'd think you'd at least have the guts to confront me to my face. Why are you doing this? You haven't hurt my dog, have you?" Surely even Todd wouldn't do that. Would he?

"I have no interest in your mutt, Mary George, and I've never been inside your apartment. Believe me, if I had, you'd know it for sure. And it wouldn't be for the dog."

My throat felt dry, so dry I had trouble swallowing. "Watch out for this guy, Mary George," my friend Missy had warned me, but of course I hadn't listened. I was listening now.

When Todd spoke again, his voice, under other circumstances, might be considered a lover's whisper. "Don't you worry, my girl, I won't forget this. Or you."

I thought Doc Nichols would never get back from lunch, although he only took his usual forty-five minutes. I was even glad to see Amanda Fitzgerald and her ill-tempered cat, Snooks, whose evil fangs and claws would make a Bengal tiger think twice. By two o'clock the waiting room was jammed and I didn't have time to worry until the last patient, an energetic Laborador, led his owner to the parking lot and home.

"Try not to think about it, Sport. We're going to find that funny old dog of yours." Doc Nichols watched me from the door of the examining room as I gathered my things at the end of the day. It was after six and I usually left a half hour before that. He shook his head and smiled. "You know nobody's gonna want that dog but you. He'll turn up."

I knew he was trying to make me smile, so I did. I had called Animal Control three times, and we'd been in touch with the microchip company to see if Hairy had been turned in at a shelter, but so far, no luck.

"Give it some time," the doc said, briskly drying his hands. "He's only been missing since yesterday. Who knows, when you get home, you might just find a big, brown dog waiting on your doorstep."

But what if he wasn't? I dreaded going back to those three empty rooms. Even Augusta had deserted me, and the weather didn't cooperate either. Just as I reached our street, thunder rumbled and black clouds turned day into night. If Hairy were there he would hear my car in the drive and gallop to meet me. Oh, how I wanted to see his big, raggedy shape!

But Hairy Brown wasn't there. Instead someone else waited under the small overhang by the door. Someone tall. A man. And in the shadows I couldn't see his face.

# CHAPTER 12

HE WAVED AND STARTED TOWARD ME AT A HALF RUN. I didn't have room to turn around without running over him, and it was raining so hard I couldn't see to back down the drive. I locked my doors as I threw on the brakes, scattering gravel left and right. If Todd wanted to reach me, he'd have to break a window.

"Mary George?" Someone tapped on the window glass. He had something oblong in his other hand, and with a snap it ballooned into something round.

"Thought you might need an umbrella," Kent Coffey said. "Watch your step. There's a puddle here."

Sheepishly, I unlocked my door, and with his arm to steady me, stepped into the mire. I was glad the rain hid my burning face.

"Heard about your break-in yesterday," Kent said as he waited for me to unlock my front door. "Hairy turned up yet?"

I shook my head. "No, and I can't imagine where he is. Looks like he just disappeared." I wanted to cry. Instead I went into the bathroom and wrapped my wet hair in a towel.

I found Kent flipping through a magazine in the living room, looking about him as if he might be disappointed. "Did you expect to see the grisly scene of the crime?" I asked, tucking my towel into a turban.

"From what Miss Fronie said, I thought maybe Ma Barker and the boys had dropped by." Kent tossed aside his magazine and sat beside me. "Sure surprised me! I might've walked in on your mystery guest yesterday if I hadn't been in a hurry to keep an appointment."

"What do you mean?"

"I came home for a few minutes to get a report I needed, and was on my way out when I heard somebody down here. I just thought it was you. Still, I wondered why you were home in the middle of the afternoon." Kent frowned. "Started to stop by, ask if you were sick, if I could bring you something, but then I thought if you really felt bad, you'd rather not be bothered."

It couldn't have been Robbie. Our young neighbor said he fed and exercised the dog around noon. "What about the dog?" I said. "Did you hear Hairy?"

He closed his eyes. "Hairy. No, I don't believe I did. He didn't bark or growl, anything like that."

He wouldn't, of course. "Was there a car? Whoever was here must've had some kind of transportation."

"Didn't notice any, but he could have parked on the street. Neighbors wouldn't pay much attention to a car parked on a public street."

I didn't say anything. Couldn't. It hit me like a splash of ice water how frightened I was. When Kent went back to his own apartment I would be alone, and although I no longer kept a key under the loose brick out front, it wouldn't take a magician to get inside. I examined my fingernails, gnawed to nubs, and curled them into fists. Why was Todd doing this to me? What did he want?

Kent touched my arm with what was probably meant to be a reassuring touch and I had to force myself not to jump away from him. *What if the intruder hadn't been Todd?* I didn't know if that was good or bad.

"I suppose you've checked the animal shelters?" Kent leaned back to took at me. He must have read my message as he didn't try to touch me.

"And all the vets within a hundred miles. Nothing."

"Then let's go take a look around." This time he did grab my hand.

"Where?" I let him pull me to my feet. The towel slipped to the floor.

"Here. Troublesome Creek. Anywhere. We'll grab some hamburgers. I'll drive, and you look. Maybe we'll see him, maybe not. At least we'll be doing something." He threw the towel at me and waited by the door. "Hurry and get ready. I'm starving."

I dried my hair and put on jeans and a baggy blue shirt. This man was almost as bossy as Augusta, but for some reason I didn't resent it. After all, he was just trying to help. God knows, I needed it! Kent was right:

at least we'd be doing *something*. And I wasn't completely unaware that the rain had made my hair curl just a little around my face and that the blue of my shirt was the color of Kent Coffey's eyes.

We drove in gloomy drizzle for most of two hours, cruising past back alleys, vacant lots, trash collection sites where stray animals usually hang out. Three or four scavenging dogs scattered when our headlights circled the parking lot behind Anderson's Market, but none of them was Hairy Brown.

The rain had slacked when we pulled in front of Earl's Quick Trip for gas, and as Kent went inside to pay, I saw Delia Sims coming out with a sack in her hand. I called to her and waved from where I waited in the car.

"Mary George, is that you? Whose car?" She frowned as she looked it over.

I explained about Kent, and then about Hairy Brown since she hadn't heard what had happened. "He's not anywhere in town," I said. "We've looked everywhere we could think of—and then some."

"Oh, honey, I'm sorry." Delia reached in the window and took my hand, and the sweet, familiar touch of an old friend made me wilt a little. "I'm afraid something awful's happened to him." I sniffed, searching for a tissue.

Cans clanked as she shifted the sack to her other arm, patted her pockets. "You say your apartment was disturbed. Was anything else missing?"

"Not that I could tell."

"I just thank the good Lord you're all right, Mary George Murphy! I hope you've locked that place up tight." Delia put her head to one side and looked at me with her big old worried brown eyes. "You know you can stay with me."

"Thanks, but I'll be fine. Miss Fronie's close by, and Kent's just upstairs. It's not like I'm there all alone," I dried my eyes on the tail of my shirt.

She clutched the bag closer and made that little cat-sneeze sound that means she doesn't put much significance to what I said. "You know what he's after, don't you?" Delia said. "Somebody's looking for that Bible, Mary George."

"Well, they're looking in the wrong place. I don't have it. It might help, though if I could get my hands on that cookie jar. Surely that woman's due back from Europe soon. I've tried and tried to call her. Just how long a tour is she taking?"

"I imagine she'll be back any day now. Her cousin should know; if you like, I'll give Lottie a call tomorrow." Delia peered closer. "But what makes you think having that cookie jar will bring you any closer to finding the Bible?"

"I just know Aunt Caroline meant for me to have it, that's all. Guess I'll know more when I find it." How could I say more? The ceramic dog had been the first thing I'd noticed in the attic after Aunt Caroline died. Set apart from everything else, it was as if she had meant it as a sign. And even then, I didn't realize its significance until it worked its way into my dreams. I had dreamed of the ceramic dog for the third time the night before. This time I was decorating cookies to fill the jar, sprinkling sugar crystals over a large ginger-bread angel. Only it wasn't Aunt Caroline who was helping me but my grandmother, who died when I was four, and whose face I barely remembered. Yet I knew it was my grandmother.

"Are you absolutely sure you don't have that Bible?" Delia insisted. "Could Caroline have put it inside something? Maybe it's in another cover."

"Why would she do that?" I couldn't imagine why anybody would be interested in that old Bible in the first place, but the facts screamed out. Somebody wanted *something* badly enough to search my things—maybe even enough to kill.

"At first I thought it was Todd, but now I'm not so sure." I told Delia how my ex-fiancé had stalked me the day before. "He denies it, of course, and he could be telling the truth, but he says things—threatening things. I'm not kidding, Delia, this guy gives me the creeps."

"Who gives you the creeps?" Kent opened the door on the driver's side and slid in beside me, depositing a six-pack between us. "Thought I might talk you into coming up for a beer?"

Delia stuck her head in my window and gave him the once-over. I introduced the two of them in the manner Aunt Caroline had taught me, but when Kent smiled and reached across me to offer his hand, Delia backed quickly away, barely acknowledging it.

"Better go," she said. "Ran clean out of cat food—that's why I'm here—and the kitties are waiting. Can't let my babies go hungry." She gave the car door a final thump before turning away. "I'll call you tomorrow, Mary George."

It sounded like a warning.

"What was that all about?" Kent asked as we drove away.

"What do you mean?"

"Oh, come on, don't pretend! That woman back there—your friend. Is my fly unzipped, or was it something I said?"

101

I laughed and glanced over to check that out. "No to both questions. I think Delia's getting a little uptight about moving. She's lived in that house forever, and then she found out they don't permit pets at that Pine Thicket place. Frankly, I think she has condo-itis!"

My answer seemed to satisfy him, but it didn't convince me. It wasn't like my old neighbor to do something like that. She had acted skittish, almost rude. Not like Delia at all.

"Did you leave your stereo on?" Kent asked when we got back to Miss Fronie's. Benny Goodman or Duke Ellington—somebody—was swinging out with "On the Atchison, Topeka and the Santa Fe."

I smiled in the darkness as we walked up the narrow flagstone path to my door. Augusta did like those train songs.

"Where have you been?" I demanded when I was sure Kent was upstairs and out of hearing. Since it was getting kind of late and we both had to work the next day, Kent and I decided to socialize tomorrow night instead, and I'd promised him dinner as well.

"Oh, good. That must mean you missed me." Augusta grabbed my hands and whirled me about until I felt like one of those china ballerinas on top of a music box.

" '*Miss you since you went away . . . miss you more than words can say . .*.'" Augusta sang, finally settling against the cushions of the couch with her dainty feet crossed. She wasn't even breathing hard. "Goodness, haven't thought of that song in years! We heard it just about every day when I was here last."

I panted, waiting for the room to stop whirling. "You didn't answer my question," I said.

"Look, Mary George, I know I can be a bit of a dose

102

at times. I thought you needed a break, that's all."

I made a face. "And you didn't? You really picked a great time to disappear. Somebody came in here while we were out yesterday and tore the place up looking for something, and I haven't seen Hairy since." I sank down beside her and put my face in my hands. "Kent and I have been out looking for him for hours, and I've checked everywhere. He could be lying out by the side of the road somewhere, you know what a klutz he is." My head felt like it weighed a ton and I rested it against the back of the sofa.

"I don't think so," Augusta said.

"How do you know?" I heard her move, felt myself being covered with my aunt's soft afghan, but I couldn't open my eyes.

"Trust me," Augusta said, and the last thing I remember was the scent of those heavenly strawberries.

I woke refreshed the next morning, still on the sofa, to the smell of coffee brewing and made it to work almost fifteen minutes early. Augusta had sprinkled her shoes with something that looked like—but surely couldn't be—stardust, and while they dried, padded about with bare feet happily humming the song. I didn't know if she'd be there when I got back.

I was checking the classifieds about midmorning to see if they ran my lost-dog ad when Delia appeared like a wraith before me. The Chihuahua in the kennel behind me was yapping so constantly I hadn't even heard her come in.

A strand of her usually tidy white hair trailed across one cheek, and something that looked like snow drifted down the front of her dress. "Now I know where I've seen that man, Mary George! It just came to me all of a sudden-like when I was rolling out pie crust for the picnic tomorrow. You know how Caroline loved peach cobbler . . . it was one of her favorites, and that's what made me think of it."

"Think of what? What man?" I tried to whisper because Royce Bolding was sitting right there under my nose with his accident-prone collie pup, and what Royce doesn't know hasn't happened yet.

"That man you were with last night—the one who lives· upstairs at Fronie's. He's the one I saw at your aunt's last spring, the one I told you about."

I rattled the newspaper, hid behind it, trying not to smile. "Delia, you must be mistaken. What would Kent Coffey be doing at Aunt Caroline's? Why, he didn't even know her."

She narrowed her eyes at me, clamped that mouth tight as an oyster, and leaned as far as she could over the counter. "And how do you know that, Mary George? Do you think he's about to admit it?" My neighbor reared back and got a second wind. "And I'll tell you something else: his car looked familiar too. Thought I'd seen it somewhere before, and I have. *Parked right over there in Caroline's driveway.*"

There was something about the way she said it that made me stop smiling. Delia Sims will indulge in gossip as much as the next person, but she's not one to embellish, and I've never known her to tell an out-and-out lie. Still I asked, "Are you sure about this?"

"If I wasn't sure, I wouldn't be standing here," she said. "That man is up to no good."

# CHAPTER 13

"YOU ARE COMING TO THE PICNIC SATURDAY?" DELIA said. "Sounds almost like old times. A blue grass group's supposed to play in the bandstand and there'll be a costume parade in the park."

"Wouldn't miss it," I said. I didn't tell her I would be accompanied by her current suspect or that I was cooking his dinner tonight. That wouldn't do at all.

The picnic is the annual Fourth of July celebration sponsored by the 'I'll Try Society,' a group of citizens who began as sort of a literary club in the early part of the century. Most of them "inherited" their memberships, I think. Aunt Caroline belonged and so does Delia—as did their parents before them, and so on. The official name for the festivities is the Star Spangled Freedom Festival, but everybody just calls it the picnic.

"I hope you're going to keep an eye out for that Kent person," Delia said. "I don't like him living so close. It's just too, too convenient."

"I'm sure he'll be glad to move if we ask him," I said.

"Joke if you will, Mary George, but I'm asking Fronie about him. Surely she must know something about the man's background."

"Wait, don't . . . I'll do it. We don't want to make him suspicious, and you know how obvious Fronie can be. Just give me a couple of days. Maybe I can find out what he was doing at Aunt Caroline's. Could be something perfectly innocent."

She made that cat-sneeze sound again. "You just be careful, Mary George. A lot can happen in a couple of days."

I had just started to tell her about almost finding Sam, when a woman and two crying children rushed in with a kitten that had darted in front of their car and I had to give Doc a hand. I still had the slip of paper Sam's old teacher had given me with his name and address; I kept it tucked inside my billfold with a sixpence Uncle Henry gave me, but I couldn't work up the courage to call.

Because of the emergency, I didn't get home as early as I'd hoped. The kitten had used one of its nine lives, Doc Nichols said, but it should be good for the remaining eight. By the time he finished seeing the rest of his patients, it was after five o'clock, and Kent was due at my place at seven.

I tried not to break any traffic laws as I drove home. If I hurried, I had at least thirty minutes to snoop around inside Kent Coffey's apartment before he came home to change for dinner.

The extra key hung on a small nail to one side of his door as I knew it did. He had told me about it the day before. I felt a small, nagging sense of guilt for betraying a trust, but that's all it was—small—like an annoying housefly buzzing about my face. I brushed it away and let myself inside. Augusta wouldn't approve, so I didn't bother to let her know what I was doing. Of course that didn't mean she *didn't,* but so far, so good.

I noticed the smell at once. Fresh paint—the oil-based kind—and was careful not to touch the walls. Funny. Kent hadn't mentioned having his apartment painted. Enough light came from the windows to see that the living room furniture wasn't covered with drop cloths, and pictures still hung on the walls. Must be another room. Shutting the door behind me, I moved on, stopping to take off my shoes in case Miss Fronie might

106

be listening.

His kitchen was neater than mine. Clean dishes dried in a rack by the sink. Curtains made of red checkered dish towels hung above it. The refrigerator contained a carton of milk, eggs, half a cantaloupe, lettuce droopy enough to wrap presents in, and a week's supply of beer. Boxes of frozen dinners filled the freezer. Nothing here.

Kent's floor plan was the reverse of mine, so his bedroom should be above my living area. The smell of paint was stronger here, and the door was open so I ventured in. Aside from a couple of tables against the wall and an old kitchen chair with a broken back, the room was empty of furniture. Built-in shelves held tubes of paint, brushes, thinner, stacks of canvases. Others leaned against the walls. Two large easels stood near the window. One contained an unfinished painting of an old woman sitting in a porch rocker looking with longing at a rusting mailbox. You could tell by the expression on her face she didn't expect any mail. A photograph of the same woman was fastened to the canvas.

The other painting was covered by a paint-smeared cloth.

I looked at my watch. Kent was usually home by six-fifteen. It was almost ten after six. Carefully I lifted the rag from the painting.

Aunt Caroline's face looked back at me.

She was wearing her "good" rose print dress with the white lace collar, the one we had buried her in. The artist had painted her seated by the piano at home with one hand on the keyboard and the other in her lap, and she looked so real I wanted to throw my arms around her.

"I was going to ask you to take a look at it after I'd

added the final touches, but now that you'd found your way in, maybe you'd like to volunteer an opinion." Kent Coffey stood in the doorway behind me. I had no idea how long he had been there.

"And an explanation as well," I said, wondering if he could hear my heart ticking away like my aunt's metronome gone wild. Even my words sounded choppy. I was breathing much too fast. "Look, Kent, I'm sorry. I have no business here, I know, but . . ."

He was looking at my bare feet and I followed his gaze. My shoes dangled from my hand. What on earth could I say? Make up some excuse like, *I came to borrow an onion?*

"I came to borrow an onion," I said. "For the spaghetti sauce . . . forgot to go by the store on my way home, and remembered about your key . . . hope you don't mind."

His expression told me he did mind, but it was the best excuse I could think of. I'm not a very good liar. "The painting is beautiful," I said. "Aunt Caroline would approve. Why didn't you tell me you were painting her portrait?"

"She wanted it to be a surprise." He folded his arms and looked at me. I wanted to run, bolt out the door, but I would have to squeeze past him in the doorway.

Now he made some sort of effort to smile and stepped back, as if he could read my thoughts. "The church music committee commissioned it," he said. "Your aunt was against it from the start—had a devil of a time getting her to pose for me." Kent followed me into the living room, which I supposed doubled as a sleeping room. "It's to hang in the choir room, they tell me. I believe they plan a formal dedication in September."

I looked down at the shoes in my hand and held them

behind me. "Stepped in mud," I said, remembering the puddle in the driveway. He didn't took as though he believed me.

"You didn't tell me you painted, Kent. I'm no critic, but I'm impressed. And I like the old woman and the mailbox. Anybody I know?"

"Lives in South Carolina, somewhere between Columbia and Newberry. Said she didn't mind if I took her photograph." Kent pulled off his tie, threw his jacket across the back of a chair. "Sometimes I take the back roads making sales calls. Interstates get so tiresome."

"But the painting of my aunt . . . do you do this often? How did the committee know about you?"

He grinned. "Unfortunately, not enough to make a living. Good thing I have another job. This was Fronie's idea. She recommended me." Kent's voice dropped to a whisper. "Except for the committee, nobody's supposed to know about this. Your aunt was going to tell you."

So that was why Delia hadn't known about the project. She wasn't on the church music committee; Fronie Temple was. I felt about twenty pounds lighter.

"Well," I said. "Guess I'd better start dinner!"

He waited until I reached the door. "Don't you want your onion?" Kent said.

I accepted one from the mesh bag that hung inside his broom closet, then took it home and stirred it around with some ground beef and some of that spaghetti sauce that comes in a jar. After a couple of glasses of wine, it tasted pretty good. The whole time Kent was in my apartment I worried about him wandering into my kitchen and finding the bag of onions I kept in a bin under my counter.

And I worried about Augusta Goodnight too. She was there somewhere, I was sure of it, and I couldn't relax.

After all, here I was entertaining a good-looking man for dinner, complete with wine, salad, and a really good cheesecake from the frozen food section. Kent apparently had forgiven me for invading his secret studio, and it should have been a special evening, even if I did cheat on the spaghetti sauce.

It wasn't. I found it almost impossible to get into serious necking with an angel looking over my shoulder. And I'll admit I had one ear tuned to the telephone in case someone answered my ad. One lady called after dinner about a white poodle she'd found that, according to her, was "dirty enough to be brown," and later a man phoned to tell me he'd seen a dog like Hairy—only it was a month ago. Naturally, every time the phone rang, my hopes soared, then fell with a splat!

Still, the two of us were cuddled on the sofa watching a movie on TV when Delia phoned. The movie was that old Hitchcock thriller, the one where Cary Grant hides in a cornfield from a sniper in a crop-dusting plane, and I could watch it over and over. But tonight I just couldn't get comfortable with this relationship. I knew it, and Kent Coffey knew it too.

His arm was around me, my head rested on his shoulder, his lips were about two inches away, and he smelled wonderful. I closed my eyes and saw Sam, the Sam of my childhood. What would he look like now? And what if he was married?

But what if he wasn't?

I was relieved when the telephone rang.

"Mary George," Delia Sims said. "Are you alone? Can we talk?"

"No and no," I told her. "I'll call you back, okay?"

"Look," Kent said as I hung up the phone. "I can see you have something on your mind, and to tell you the

110

truth, I've had a tough week. Why don't we take up where we left off another night?" He kissed me lightly on the lips, thanked me for his dinner, and disappeared almost as magically as Saint Nicholas on Christmas Eve. Only Kent Coffey wasn't Santa, and it wasn't even December. I guess he had had just about enough of me, and I can't say I blamed him. We seemed to be making a habit of postponing evenings together.

"Don't forget the picnic tomorrow," I called after him as he left, but I don't think he heard me. At least, that's what I chose to think.

"Did I interrupt something?" Delia asked when I phoned her back. "If it was that Kent Coffey, I'm not sorry!"

"Well, you should be! Not that you interrupted anything with any kind of future to it. But you've got this poor guy all wrong, Delia. Kent Coffey had a perfect excuse for visiting Aunt Caroline." I told her about the painting.

"A little too perfect if you ask me," Delia said. "So what if he did paint her portrait? Does that rule him out from being a suspect in her death? Maybe he got greedy, wanted more for the portrait than Caroline could afford. He can't be making much of a living or he wouldn't be living at Fronie's."

"Thanks a lot," I said. "Delia, you know Aunt Caroline didn't have money for things like that, and wouldn't spend it on herself if she did. The church music committee commissioned that painting, and we're not supposed to know a thing about it, so please don't let on to Fronie Temple that I told you."

I could tell I'd said the right thing. Delia practically purred. It did her heart good to be one up on Fronie.

"Well, I hope she's happy! That woman's been

111

wanting to head up some committee or other ever since she came here. But never mind about Fronie. What's this you were fixing to tell me this morning about that old friend of yours? Sam, wasn't it? Have you seen him? Did he remember you?"

"I haven't exactly *seen* him yet," I admitted. "But at least now I know where I can find him." I told her about my conversation with Geraldine Thompson.

Delia hesitated before she spoke again. "Sometimes I wonder about you, Mary George Murphy," she said. "And I wouldn't let my guard down just yet around that Coffey fellow either. He may know more than he lets on. Just you remember that."

"Uh-huh," I said. "By the way, did you have a chance to call Lottie Greeson about when the Shugarts will be home?"

"They're staying a few extra days in London. Should be home by the end of the week." Delia paused. "Mary George, I may be an old butt-in, but I don't feel right about that man you're seeing—portrait or no portrait. Now, promise me you'll be careful."

"Promise," I said, laughing. "See you at the picnic tomorrow."

But after I hung up, I double locked the doors. Silence hung heavy outside my windows, and the shadows seemed deeper than usual in this old, high-ceilinged place. Hairy Brown wasn't much of a watch dog, but I missed him more than ever tonight.

Then from the kitchen came the unmistakable smell of hot chocolate, and through the doorway I saw Augusta stirring a simmering pan on the stove. For a while, at least, I would have my very own angel.

# CHAPTER 14

IT'S ALWAYS HOT IN TROUBLESOME CREEK ON THE Fourth of July. Today was no exception. Petunias growing in a tangle beside Miss Fronie's narrow walk hung their pink and purple heads and shriveled in the sun. Heat rose in shimmering waves from the sidewalk. I wore the nearest thing to nothing I could find—shorts and a baggy, sleeveless shirt. A wide-brimmed straw hat kept the sun from my face as Kent and I walked the few blocks to Nathan P. Treadway Park where the festivities were to take place. Nathan P. Treadway has been dead for at least fifty years. He donated the land for the park to the city, fought in the First World War, and made a lot of money in the insurance business—although not in that order. A pudgy statue of him stands at the corner of the park next to the Civil War cannon. Aunt Caroline said he's supposed to be thinking, but he looks like he's picking his nose to me.

I had spent the morning cutting crusts from pimento cheese sandwiches just the way my aunt had taught me. I had a selection of fruits . . . well, okay . . . two different kinds of grapes and a couple of apples, and Augusta had baked nut-filled brownies. She'd eaten almost half of them, but there were still enough for my date and me to share.

Kent Coffey, cooler in hand, had turned up on my doorstep at a quarter till four, just as he'd said he would, and neither of us mentioned the awkwardness of the night before. Now we threaded our way through sweaty, red-faced bodies, hands almost touching on the handle of the wicker basket. A crowd had gathered around the old cannon, which was jammed with wads of newspaper

113

and gunpowder and fired every July Fourth, causing elderly ladies to scream and jump, and dogs to run howling under porches. Last year the blast had cracked the plate glass window of *The Troublesome Creek Banner,* our weekly newspaper. Today, the editor, a Yankee who had come here from what Delia refers to as "up the road a piece," stood out front waving a white flag on a stick.

Delia Sims hollered to me from a bunting-draped booth where she sold cookbooks for the Culpeper County Humane Society. I know she expected me to drag Kent over so she could scan him with her built-in suspicious-person detector, but I pretended to be in a hurry. Actually I was. One spot remained in the shade of the tulip poplar on the other side of the park, and we claimed it seconds before a family arrived with purposeful intent from the opposite direction.

It wasn't until we were almost eye to eye that I recognized Bonita Moody.

"Mary George Murphy," I said, feeling a little sheepish about grabbing the only shade. I extended my hand and waited for her to introduce her family. She didn't. "Look," I said, glancing at the few inches of unclaimed space, "maybe we can all squeeze in . . ."

"No. No thanks, that's all right. I think I see a place over by the fountain . . . better hurry!" And off she went. Her eyes had warned me to keep my mouth shut. For heaven's sake, was the silly woman still afraid to tell her husband about the secret piano lessons?

The cannon boomed with its usual deafening roar, spewing confetti across the grass, and the editor, his window intact, retired his flag of truce for another year.

Having staked our space in the shade, Kent and I wandered about the park making an effort to stay in the shadows. In the bandstand, pink-clad five-year-olds from Miss Lillian's School of Dance shuffled dutifully to "The Sidewalks of New York" and the local gymnastics team bounced and flipped on a trampoline under the sycamore's spreading limbs. Watching them, I had a peculiar feeling someone was staring at me, but the couple behind us were desperately scrambling to keep three unruly grandchildren under control, and the large woman on my right concentrated on eating her ice cream before it ran down her arm. Nobody paid the slightest attention to me. Still, the awareness persisted, and it made me uneasy. I wished it would go away. Even the statue of old Nathan seemed to glare at me— still pissed, I guess, from that Halloween night I'd rolled him with toilet paper.

Maybe I was becoming paranoid, but somebody *had* followed me to Hughes earlier in the week, and my apartment had been invaded while I was away. Still, I didn't mention it to my date. This was supposed to be a fun day, sort of a new beginning for us, and I had a slight suspicion he probably thought I was nuts already.

By the time Kent and I had watched the watermelon-eating contest and the last of the costume parade tottered past, it was getting time to eat. The couple behind us were about two thighs and a drumstick into a carton of fried chicken, and nearby somebody cooked burgers on a portable grill. The aromas dueled for attention. Kent rubbed his hands together and smiled. "Well," he said, "'let's see what we have. I can hardly wait."

"Yes, you can," I told him. I opened our basket and came face-to-face with the bland white triangles that would be our meal. A plump shadow ballooned over us, and I jumped, thinking the mysterious person who'd

115

been following me was making a move at last.

"So here you are!" Fronie Temple stood before us, resplendent in floral shirt and pants, her bright hair held back with a pink terry cloth band. Like an offering, she bore in front of her on a paper plate something that resembled hair balls that quivered and glistened with grease. Now she shoved this disgusting mound before us.

"Squash morsels, made'm myself. Didn't come out quite the way they were supposed to, but they taste okay. Thought you might like some."

I've seen road kill that looked more appetizing. "Why, thanks, Miss Fronie," I said, not daring to meet Kent's eyes. It was easier than refusing and we could bury it when she left. I offered my hamper. "Care for a sandwich?"

"My goodness, no, thank you, dear. Have to watch what I eat. Besides, I'm due to help out at the Women's Club tent. We're having a bake sale, you know."

Kent and I covered the offending plate with a paper napkin shroud and delved into the sandwiches as soon as she was out of sight. I don't ever remember them tasting as good.

I was on my second brownie when I heard a man's loud voice. "Why in the world did you do that, Bonita? I've told you—"

"But I didn't mean to! Look, I didn't know she was—" Bonita Moody must have realized she was raising her voice because she didn't finish what she was going to say. Obviously her husband wasn't pleased with something she had done. I wondered if it had anything to do with taking piano lessons from my aunt.

The Moodys had abandoned their spot by the fountain when I strolled by a few minutes later, leaving Kent

116

napping in the shade. Guilt for ignoring Delia was beginning to nag at me, and I looked for her at the booth where I'd seen her last, but she wasn't there. I bought a cookbook from the Humane Society and a pink geranium from the Future Farmers and stopped to watch a group of children chasing one another around the bandstand while the blue grass group tuned up for the concert. The sun was still hot, but shadows were growing longer and a small breeze lifted moist hair from my face.

I'm sure I must have yelled when a firm hand clamped suddenly on my shoulder. "Why'd you run off like that, Mary George?" Delia shouted in my ear. "I couldn't take off and chase after you, and there's somebody here looking for you."

"Huh? Who's that?"

"Some young man, didn't give his name. Said somebody told him I'd know where he could find you."

My first thought was that someone had found Hairy Brown. "Where did he go? Did he say where he would be? Did he mention anything about my dog?"

"No, just said he'd try to get back in touch if he didn't find you. Never said what he wanted."

That didn't sound so good. That must be why I felt I was being watched, but why didn't the man say something? Introduce himself? "Delia, what did this guy look like? Do you see him anywhere around here now?"

I must have grabbed her arm, because she made a point of rubbing it as she frowned at me. "What's the matter with you, Mary George? If I were you, I'd be more concerned about that Kent person you came with. I asked Fronie about him, you know, and she knows absolutely nothing about the man—or so she says. Acts like she's keeping something back if you ask me."

117

"You didn't tell her you knew about the painting? Delia, you promised!"

"Oh, of course not! Shh, wait a minute now. The quartet's fixing to sing."

We listened to the foursome sing that rendition of "Elizabeth" the Statler Brothers made popular, and I started looking around for Kent. Apparently Delia didn't find this stranger particularly threatening, but after all the things that had been happening lately, I'd feel more secure if Kent were around.

I found him eating the last of the brownies and washing it down with what had to be lukewarm beer. He didn't seem to notice I'd been gone. And then I saw he was talking with someone; a tall, sandy-haired man in blue denim shorts stood leaning against the tree. He wore a T-shirt that said I Brake for Food on the back and he had on the rattiest-looking moccasins I've ever seen.

Kent grinned when he saw me and licked a chocolate crumb from his fingers. "Mary George, I've been talking with an old friend of yours here—"

Just then the guy in the T-shirt turned, and the first thing I saw was a decal of an enormous hamburger on the front of his shirt, then above that, his face. An open, good-natured face with a light scattering of freckles, pond green eyes, and a wide mouth that smiled at me. I smiled back.

"Mary G., I'm Sam," the man said. He started to stretch out a hand, then changed his mind and held out his arms.

"I know," I said, and walked right into them, held on tight. I think I cried, and for a minute I closed my eyes and felt myself soar free: away from the hot, crowded park, the amplified sound of guitars, to a brown path by

118

a quiet creek. I took a deep breath, liking the way his shoulder felt beneath my cheek. He smelled like chili and onions.

"How did you know where you could find me?" I asked when I could talk.

He held me away and looked at me, then hugged me again. "My old teacher, Mrs. Thompson. You gave her your address, remember?"

"Yes, but how did you know I was here—in the park?"

Sam laughed, and he looked about eight years old again. "Don't tell me you're that forgetful already, Mary G.! You left a note on your door."

But I hadn't. Had I? I glanced at Kent who sat watching us with a puzzled smile. "Did I? Did you?" He shook his head. Maybe Miss Fronie had put it there in case someone answered my ad in the paper.

"I heard about your aunt's death," Sam said. "I'm sorry, Mary G. What an awful thing to happen!"

*If only you knew*, I thought. "She was the only mother I remember," I said. "Everybody loved Aunt Caroline." *Everybody, that is, except for one.*

Sam joined us on the blanket and ate the handful of grapes left in the basket. "I've tried and tried to find you," he told me. "I can't believe this is really you, that we're actually sitting here together. Your friend Delia told me you were pretty, Mary G., and darned if she's not right. Guess I was expecting a tall, skinny kid in braids."

I laughed. "Are you trying to tell me I was an ugly duckling?"

"No, you were a short, skinny kid in braids. To be honest, I had a hard time recognizing you. Wasn't sure I had the right one until I worked up enough courage to ask Kent here."

"Please tell me you've been watching me all afternoon," I said. "Then maybe I won't feel so spooked."

Sam finished the grapes and hunted for more. "Okay. I've been watching you all afternoon—well, off and on. Wanted to be sure you were *the* Mary George Murphy I used to know. Sounds like a line, you'll have to admit: 'Pardon me, but haven't we met before? Like about a million years ago in another lifetime?' "

He told me about his teaching job in Salisbury and the volunteer work he was doing at the camp. "We're really shorthanded out there if you have any time to spare," Sam said. "Of course, when you get down to it, we need money more than anything else—and somebody who knows what to do with it."

I grinned. "I know what to do with it . . . I think. I've just never had a chance to find out."

"Mary G., you wouldn't recognize the old place," Sam said. "You oughta come out and see it."

I wasn't about to tell him I already had. "I think he's trying to put me to work," I said to Kent, who wasn't looking all that pleased with the situation, and I couldn't blame him. I was about to ask him if he was ready to leave when Delia wandered up carrying a box of leftover cookbooks, which she dropped with a thud.

"Ah, I see you two found each other," she said with a sly little grin. She made it sound like something out of a cheap romance novel. I introduced the three of them, trying my best to remember my manners in a sticky situation. I'd like nothing more than to spend the rest of the evening talking with Sam, but it wouldn't be fair to Kent. I had to do something.

Delia's eyes widened. "This is Sam? *The* Sam?"

If she would just read my look, she'd know I'd like her to cool it with the *the* Sam bit, but apparently Delia was look illiterate. Now she opened her mouth to continue.

I jumped in with both feet. "Sam was telling us about his work at Summerwood," I said, giving Kent a silent signal to slip away. "Why don't you tell her about it, Sam?"

Naturally he latched on to that like a dog to the mailman's leg, and we left them there talking together. Sam waved to me as we walked away. "I'll call you tomorrow," he said. It was almost impossible to hide my pleasure.

It didn't occur to me until we were almost home that I hadn't thought to ask Sam about his marital status. And I still couldn't figure out how he'd known where to look for me. "Are you sure you didn't leave a note on the door when we left?" I asked Kent again.

"Absolutely." He shook his head and glanced at me with a puzzled look. The two of us walked slowly, not saying much, the empty basket bumped our legs with each step. Finally Kent pointed to something as we came within sight of my door, and his voice sounded rocking-chair weary. "There's your note, Mary George. You must've put it there at the last minute. Guess you just forgot."

The message was written primly on a small piece of white paper: Gone to Picnic in Park. And it was signed with my name, only I didn't write it.

And there at the top—so faint I could barely see it— was a slight smudge of chocolate.

# CHAPTER 15

I INVITED KENT IN FOR A COOL DRINK, WHICH HE politely declined. I was glad. "I'm sorry," I said, and kissed his cheek. I was saying good-bye and he knew it. I walked inside feeling more than a little puzzled with myself, and put my empty basket in the kitchen. It had been a most peculiar day. A handsome, likable man had demonstrated an obvious interest in me, and I had just opened the door and showed him the way out without even a second thought. And all because of Sam. I hadn't seen Sam since he had corrected my table manners and then told me he was leaving me all practically in the same breath. That was almost twenty years ago. A lot can happen to change a person in twenty years. For all I knew Sam could have a wife and six kids. He might even be an ax murderer. But he didn't look like an ax murderer.

The apartment seemed quieter than usual. Augusta had left her brief note on my door and taken flight, and Hairy's favorite rug lay empty and undisturbed beside my bed. His water dish waited in the kitchen. I checked my answering machine, but no one had called.

In the bedroom the good-luck rock frog Sam had given me crouched on my dresser and leered at me with its funny goldpainted eyes. I smiled, wondering if Sam would remember.

The temperature had *dropped* to a sweltering eighty-five degrees and my air conditioner groaned under the stress. I stripped off my sticky clothes and spent at least ten minutes in the shower washing hamburger smoke from my hair. The phone was ringing when I stepped out and I hurried to answer it, hoping it would be Sam.

It was. "I couldn't wait till tomorrow," Sam said.

"Where are you? How did you get home so fast?" I looked at the clock. It was a little before nine.

"I'm at Delia's," he said. "Are you alone?"

"Well . . . yes. How did you know?"

"I didn't know, I just hoped," Sam admitted. "Delia's kindly offered to put me up for the night. We're sitting out here on her porch having a beer—or at least I'm having a beer. Delia's drinking something with ice in it, and she says she'll make one for you if you'll come over."

My hair was dripping down my neck, I was tired, and had nothing exciting to wear. "Be there in a minute," I said.

This was met by such a long silence, I thought he'd changed his mind. "Better still," Sam said at last, "why don't I come over there? We have a lot of catching up to do, and Delia says she'll leave the door unlocked for me."

I immediately scrambled for the hair dryer. "You know where to find me," I told him.

Sam Maguire stood in my small living room and looked about. It had taken him just under six minutes to get here—barely time enough for me to find a decent pair of clean shorts, put on a touch of lipstick, and comb through my damp hair.

"Smells good in here," he said.

"We've—I've been baking brownies," I said. "Sorry there aren't any left."

"Nope, not brownies." Sam frowned, sniffed. "Strawberries. Is that some kind of air freshnener? Smells like the real thing."

"Yes, doesn't it?"

123

He looked at me through narrowed eyes. "You're teasing me, Mary G."

How could he know? How could he still know after all these years when I wasn't quite telling the truth?

"Delia tells me you've been having a tough time of it, but you look terrific. There's something . . . can't quite put my finger on it . . . almost tranquil about you, about this place." Sam put an arm around me, hugged me to him. "I just have a feeling, Mary G. Everything's going to work out all right."

I wish I could be sure of the same. We sat in the living room, which was about as comfortable as the small window air conditioner could make it, and I told him about Aunt Caroline's death, what I suspected.

"You sound pretty certain about this," he said. "From what I've heard about her, your aunt doesn't sound like the type to make enemies. Could it be because of something she saw, or knew?"

"I think it was something she had, something that belonged to me." I told him about the Bible. "And a few days ago somebody came in here looking for something while I was gone—ripped my needlepoint footstool apart and rummaged through drawers. I think they were after the family Bible. Of course they didn't find it because it wasn't here."

He stretched long legs in front of him. "Any idea where it could be?"

"If I knew that, I might have some clue as to why Aunt Caroline died."

"I wonder what could be in there that somebody wants bad enough to kill for. Is there anybody you could ask? A relative or somebody?"

I shook my head. "There's nobody left but me, at least that's what my aunt always said. My parents didn't

124

have any siblings, and when they died there was no one to take me, except the home at Summerwood, until Aunt Caroline and Uncle Henry came along. And they weren't really kin, but they treated me like they were." I curled, shoeless, at one end of the sofa while Sam lounged at the other with a comfortable distance between us. I had the strangest feeling that we'd never been apart.

Now he leaned forward with one arm stretched along the back of the sofa. "Look, Mary G., I don't want to scare you, but should you be living back here by yourself like this? I know you have a landlady and that guy upstairs, but what good did they do when somebody came in here and searched the place? What if you'd been here alone? You can hardly see this place from the street."

I'd thought of that, of course. More than once. "I did have a dog," I said. I told him about Hairy Brown. "I've been running an ad in the paper, but so far I haven't had any luck." I drew up my knees and sighed. "He's such a good old dog, Sam. A big, brown wad of fur with a tongue sticking out. I can't believe how much I miss him."

He reached across and took my hand, gently stroked the back of it. He didn't even have to speak. I wanted to ask him about his marital status, his love life—or the lack of it—but I was afraid to mention it. "Have you been happy?" I asked instead.

He looked thoughtful, then smiled. "Yes, I have. Teaching can be rewarding, at least some of the time— although not financially, of course. And I really would like to see something good come of Summerwood, Mary G. These kids need it, and the land is there if we can just get funding. The church dropped their

125

sponsorship after the home closed, and I just don't have the time it takes to do it justice."

"Sounds like you need a fund-raiser," I said. "A good PR person."

"Or a guardian angel," he said.

"Goodness, I'm thirsty! Want something to drink?" I jumped up and went in the kitchen for a glass of water, then stood at the sink until my smile went away. If Sam saw my face, he wouldn't leave me alone until I told him about Augusta Goodnight, and I didn't want to scare him off after being apart so long. After all, even Sam Maguire has limits as to what he might believe.

"Why don't you drive out to Summerwood with me tomorrow?" he was saying. "And bring a paintbrush. I promised them a hand sprucing up the dining hall, and Delia said she might even come and give us some decorating tips. God knows, we can use the help!"

"I wonder if Delia's made up her mind about moving to that condo?" I said, finally composed again. "I don't know what she'd do with all her things over there. And then there's that rule about pets."

"Oh, I see she hasn't told you," Sam said.

"Told me what?"

"She's changed her mind. Told me tonight she isn't going to move."

"But she was going to put her house on the market, and I know it's depressing for her looking across the street at Aunt Caroline's place. They're. making it into offices, you know. Did she say what she was going to do?"

He smiled and shook his head. "Said she'd make a decision when the time came . . . whatever that means."

It seemed to me Augusta needed to send for backup. We didn't have enough guardian angels to go around.

"What *are* you going to do?" I asked Delia the next day as she measured the windows in the big old barn of a dining hall at Summerwood. I had been painting for hours and everything on me was sunshine yellow, including most of my hair.

Delia jotted down a number and wound the tape measure around her hand. "I'll worry about that when I have to, she said.

"Can you imagine me without my babies?' She drew herself up indignantly. "Well, there are other places to live!"

I didn't know of any right offhand, but I didn't think this was the best time to remind her of that.

"Need more paint?" Sam stood behind me with a bucket and poured some into my tray. "Do you realize we're standing just about where we always used to sit, Mary G.? Pinto beans and rice. Seems we had 'em every other day!"

"Remember Cindy?" I said. "Always made us cupcakes and sticky buns." I remembered long tables of wiggling children, the clatter of knives and forks.

"And called me Sam-I-am. Always had a joke. I thought she was beautiful."

"Cookie hated her." I dipped my roller in paint.

"Naturally," Sam said, looking thoughtful. "Remember our verse? How we made everybody sick— or tried to?"  .

I nodded. "Grisly, grimy, glumpy bats, brewed and stewed in lizard fat . . ."

"With a clump of this and a lump of that," Sam added.

"Served with a hunk of sewer rat!" Laughing, we ended the "poem" together.

"I'm afraid we made a lot of the other kids sick," I said.

Sam shrugged. "Too bad they didn't want their dessert."

Since there weren't any campers at Summerwood that day, we lunched under the trees on carry-out pizza with Rose and Lyman Cummings, the couple running the camp for the summer. Lyman, chubby and bearded, looked a little like a middle-aged Santa Claus, and, according to Sam, forever had his nose in a book. His wife, in her midforties, looked to be about a size six and had the kind of complexion a teenager might envy. She seemed to have boundless energy, fueled probably by the four pieces of pizza she'd just eaten. It was hard not to hate her.

"There's nothing to stop us from having some kind of benefit right here," Rose suggested, swigging the last of her iced tea. "Something that would bring us a little ready money for repairs. At least it would be a start."

I looked at the long, sprawling building behind us. "Why not a dance? You have the space, and you know how people go in for those line dances. How about a country-western theme? Might be kind of fun. Maybe we can get that blue grass group who played in the park to donate their time."

"Why, that's a wonderful idea," Delia said. "What made you think of that, Mary George?"

"I don't know. It just came to me," I told her. I don't know why she seemed so surprised.

"Why not next month before school starts back?" Sam suggested. "If you and Rose will work out the details, Mary G., I'll take care of the promotion end, but I've got to spend some time with my family. I promised

128

Ed we'd go fishing sometime this summer."

A rock dropped in my stomach. *Ed*? Who was this Ed? What family?

"Ed's my brother—well, half brother really." Sam stretched out in the grass and pulled his cap over his eyes. Good grief, could he read my mind? "Be in the tenth grade this fall," he said. "Dad married again when I was twelve, and they're living in Atlanta now. I try to get together with them whenever I can."

"Of course," I said, and smiled, filled with goodwill now that the rock in my middle had dissolved into mush.

"Had a bad turn there for a minute, didn't you?" Delia reminded me on the way home that night. The two of us drove back in her car since Sam lived in the other direction.

It's impossible to ignore somebody when there are only two of you in a closed car. "You don't miss much," I said. "You really like him, don't you?"

"Who?" She glanced at me and laughed. "Oh, you mean Sam . . . Well, of course I do, Mary George, only not in the same way you do."

I didn't even bother to deny it.

It was dark when we reached home and neither Kent's white Honda nor Miss Fronie's old blue Buick were parked in their usual places. Delia pulled as close to my doorstep as possible to let me out, then waited while I unlocked my door. I flicked on the outside light and stood in the doorway to see that she didn't back over my landlady's petunias on her way out. I waved at her little farewell toot of the horn and turned to go inside when I heard the unmistakable sound of a footstep in the dark yard beside the house.

129

"Delia, wait!" I screamed. But it was too late, I could hear her turning into the street, well out of earshot. Rushing inside, I tried to slam the door behind me, lock it before he could follow, but my hands seemed to have lost all communication with my brain. Suddenly the door was wrenched from me, and a large hand circled my wrist. I turned and bit what felt like a finger as hard as I could while landing a kick at my attacker's ankle.

"Ow! Goddamn it, Mary George, I just want to talk!" Todd Burkholder snatched away his injured digit. I had managed to shove him outside, but he blocked my way back in. To say that my heart raced would be an understatement. I didn't know hearts could beat that fast—I don't know why I didn't pass out.

Maybe because I was mad. "You've picked a hell of a way to go about it," I said. "What in the world is the matter with you? Can't you understand? We have nothing to talk about."

For the first time I noticed his car in the deep shadows at the far end of the yard, partially screened from view by the overgrown crape myrtles beside the driveway. Todd had parked it at the top of a slight slope facing the street—for a quick getaway, I supposed.

I forced myself to space my breathing, to speak evenly. I had to get rid of him. "Look, Todd," I said. "Why don't you come by the clinic one day next week? We can talk there if you want, but this is not the time or the place. It's late—and frankly, you frightened me."

"I did?" I think he smiled. Again his hand tightened on my arm. I had a sickening feeling I had said the wrong thing.

That did it. "Damn it, go away! I never want to see you again. Get lost, asshole!" I shoved against him with all my strength, but I might as well have been pushing on a stone wall.

And then I heard it: the deliberate grinding of gravel, the sound of a car beginning to roll. Todd's car. Slowly it began to inch down the driveway, sideswiping a shrub along the way. Pine cones crunched beneath the tires.

Unfortunately he didn't seem to notice. "Excuse me," I said in as loud a voice as I could muster, "but isn't that your car?"

"Oh, my God!" Todd Burkholder vaulted from the stoop and took off running while I squeezed inside and double locked the door.

"Mary George Murphy, there's just no excuse for such filthy language!" Augusta Goodnight said beside me.

And then I could have sworn she laughed.

# CHAPTER 16

THE NEXT DAY I FOUND OUT THAT SOMEBODY HAD RUN down Bonita Moody that night in her church parking lot, and she was lying in a coma over at Culpeper General with extensive internal injuries.

I should have guessed something had happened because it took the police over an hour to check out my complaint about Todd the night before, and even then the man they sent was filling in for somebody else.

By then, of course, Todd the clod was long gone, and the investigating officer (and I use that term loosely), seemed to think I was seeking revenge after a lover's spat. I could swear out an injunction, he said, although it didn't look like I'd suffered any bodily harm. Yawning, he told me there was a law now against stalking that might keep my "boyfriend" at a distance, and if I'd

131

come down to the station he was sure they'd be glad to take care of it for me.

By then it was so late I could barely keep my eyes open, so I told him I'd be there tomorrow. After all, Todd had scurried off like a roach in the kitchen light, and I had my very own guardian angel for the remainder of the evening.

But then I didn't know yet about Bonita.

I heard it first from Fronie Temple who learned about it at church. I had slept late that morning—in spite of Augusta's little tuneful reminders. I'd heard her humming as she puttered about the living room, but it took me a while to identify the song as "The Little Brown Church in the Wildwood." Augusta's not always on key.

Anyway, I must've dozed through several stanzas before the smell of coffee brewing finally lured me out of bed, and I was outside getting the Sunday paper when Fronie pulled into her garage. I heard her car door slam and turned to find her trailing after me down the drive, face all flushed, oversized crocheted handbag dangling from one arm.

"Worst thing!" she said breathlessly. "Some woman was just about killed last night right there in the parking lot at Rising Star Church of the Lamb—you know, out on the old Charlotte Highway. They said she'd gone there to practice the piano. Now, I ask you, where can a person be safe if not in her *own church*?"

"Apparently not in the parking lot," I said, hoping no one could see me standing there in my short summer pajamas. And then a little warning bell tolled in my head. *She had gone there to practice the piano.* "Do you remember who it was?" I asked.

Fronie shifted her purse and frowned. "Why, yes, I

believe it was that same woman you asked me about, Mary George. Used to take piano lessons from Caroline. Happened after dark. Whoever hit her just drove off, they said—probably some dope dealers from out of town. Doubt if they'll ever catch them now." And my landlady shook her head until a yellow curl slipped over one eye.

I knew it wouldn't be long until Delia reported in, and sure enough, the phone rang about fifteen minutes later. Bonita had been in surgery for over three hours, she told me, and had been given several units of blood. The ministers in the community had issued an appeal on Bonita's behalf, Delia said, to replace the blood she'd used, and I couldn't think of any reason—except an intense dislike of needles—why I shouldn't donate some of my own.

Also, it might give me an opportunity to find out just how Bonita's domineering husband had reacted to her "accident." It seemed a little too much of a coincidence to me that this awful thing should happen just after I heard him reading her the riot act at the picnic a couple of days before. Bonita Moody was afraid of something, and I was pretty sure I knew what—or who—it was.

Ray Moody was either on the verge of a nervous breakdown or he was a dam good actor. I found him pacing the corridor outside his wife's hospital room while nurses changed her linen. I wore an adhesive bandage on my arm and a bright sticker that said Be Nice to Me—I Gave Blood Today! I'd had a doughnut and a carton of milk and felt just fine.

But Ray Moody didn't, or at least he didn't look fine. He looked awful. His eyes were puffy and red rimmed in a white, drawn face, and when I stopped to introduce myself I could see my words didn't register. At first.

"What was your name again?" he asked, stopping to lean against the pale green corridor wall. The man looked as if he hadn't slept in a year. I had come here prepared to blame him for what happened to Bonita. Now I wasn't so sure.

"Mary George Murphy," I repeated. "Your wife Bonita took—"

He nodded impatiently. "Piano lessons from your aunt."

"How did you know? I thought—"

"What do you mean, 'How did I know?' Bonita told me." Ray Moody glanced at the room behind him and came almost close to smiling. "Or, I should say she finally got around to telling me after that happened to your aunt. She's a funny one, Bonita is . . . Lord, if I'd known she wanted to learn that bad, we could've worked it out somehow. I should've just gone on and gotten her a keyboard or something so she wouldn't have to practice at the church." Bonita Moody's husband took out a wrinkled handkerchief and blew his nose. "That's what she was doing over there, you know. Told me she wasn't going to stay that late."

"I'm sorry," I said. "How is she?"

Head down, he rubbed his eyes, then looked away. "It don't look good, but they say she has a chance. If the preacher hadn't come by about then to get the notes for his sermon, she probably wouldn't even be alive. I think they meant to kill her."

"Did he get a look at the car?"

"Yeah, but it went screeching past him in the dark, and he didn't even see Bonita lying there until the car that hit her was gone. Says he thinks it was a Ford—gray, or maybe pate blue or white. Like I said, it was

134

dark."

Gray. The same color as Todd's Mustang. And he'd left in a huff—actually more than a huff—just before Bonita was struck. But why would Todd want to hurt Bonita Moody?

The nurse came out and nodded to him, and Ray started to go back into the room. "Wait," I said, and touched his arm. "I think your wife was afraid of something."

There, I'd said it. I began to feel a little weak. Maybe from loss of blood; maybe from being chicken hearted. Or a little of both.

He frowned. "You've got that right. I told her she should've told somebody, but Bonita—well, she was scared to talk about it."

"About what?" I asked.

Ray Moody led me aside, glanced behind him and whispered, "Look, Bonita didn't quite tell you all the truth that day you come by. She had to change her lesson day because our Margo had a dentist's appointment that Monday before your aunt died . . . It was Bonita who found her body."

I think I gasped. Somebody did. I knew someone had called for an ambulance because they reported my aunt hadn't come to the door and they couldn't get a response. It must have been Bonita Moody.

"But why was she afraid?" I asked.

"Because she thought she heard somebody in there that day. Somebody who didn't want to be seen. The front door was unlocked, so she just come in like she usually did and yelled to let your aunt know she was there. She was already dead when Bonita found her."

"Are you sure that's all?"

Ray Moody paused at the door of his wife's room.

"That's all she'll admit to, but Bonita's been acting mighty funny. I think she might've seen something too. And she forgets sometimes and talks about it—about finding her. I'm just afraid she might've mentioned it to the wrong person."

"Aren't you going to say something to the police? This might have had something to do with what happened in the parking lot. She shouldn't be left alone."

"Why do you think I'm still here? I'm just waiting for our minister to spell me so I can get a short nap. The police know all about it, but they think this was done by a teenager who'd had too much to drink." Ray Moody shook his head and I felt so sorry for him, I tasted tears trickling into my throat. "They don't pay much attention to the likes of me," he said. "We're just hoping they can find that car. The front of it oughta at least have a dent or two."

On my way home from the hospital I stopped at the Troublesome Creek police station to file my complaint against Todd Burkholder. The local police department is housed in a scruffy red brick building behind the bus station that usually isn't included on the town garden tour. I wasn't looking forward to going there, but at least things seemed to be on the quiet side.

Until I got inside. I recognized the voice first. It belonged to Mr. Hildebrand, my high school algebra teacher, and he was not pleased.

"Aunt Alma's going to be furious!" he thundered, marching back and forth in the front cubicle of an office. "And with good reason. Whoever's responsible for this should be made to pay! She's had that car three years and never put a scratch on it . . . Now this." He

136

reached the end of this three-step pace and turned abruptly. "Of course she's going to blame me. I was supposed to be keeping an eye on it while she was gone." And Walter Hildebrand, usually straitlaced and always proper, said *"Shit!"* Said it loud. And on a Sunday afternoon.

I dodged just in time to keep from being seen and clamped a hand over my mouth. Imagine! The man was human after all.

"May I help you?" A female officer greeted me from behind a counter at the far end of the room. She frowned at me, then stared until I wondered if I'd done something wrong. "Mary George, is that you?" she asked, looking closer.

That voice. I knew that voice. "Pat?" I looked at her again. "You look great! I didn't know you worked here."

"Been a long time since high school," she said. "Had to lose weight to pass the physical. I'm about thirty pounds lighter than when you last saw me."

Pat Callaghan and I had played clarinet together in the high school band, and she'd been one of those people we'd predicted "would be really pretty if she'd just lose weight." Well, she had lost weight, and Pat was a knockout.

"Do you know who that is in there?" I asked, pointing to the other room. In all the excitement, I'd forgotten for the moment why I'd come.

She laughed. "Old Starched Shorts himself! How could I forget? He's been going at it for ten minutes."

"What's going on?"

She crooked her finger, motioning me closer. "You know about that hit-and-run in a church parking lot last night? Well, looks like the car involved belonged to

Starched Shorts's Aunt Alma. Mercury Cougar. Been in her garage for about a month now while the aunt was visiting her grandchildren up in Maine, and he was supposed to keep it running, take it out now and then."

I nodded. "Only he didn't."

"Right!" Pat grinned. "Seems Walter didn't do his homework. Auntie's due home tomorrow, and when he went over there to check on the car after church today, he found the front dented and the Cougar covered in dust like it had been out in the country somewhere."

*Like to Hughes?* "Didn't he have the key? How could anybody else drive it?" I asked.

"He thinks his aunt Alma kept an extra hidden under the floor mat." Pat shrugged. "Looks like somebody else must've known about it too."

# CHAPTER 17

THE UGLY TRUTH RODE HOME LIKE A VULTURE perching on my shoulder, its claws in my flesh. It *hadn't been* Todd Burkholder who followed me to Summerwood that day, which meant he probably wasn't the one who searched my apartment and let Hairy Brown vamoose.

Still, he most definitely had harassed me, so I went ahead with the complaint. At least there was one thing I could do something about. I wondered if Todd would whine to the police about how I bit his finger.

But if not Todd, who?

I found Kent washing his car when I got home that afternoon and he gave me a friendly wave. I felt awkward at seeing him, but, living in the same house there was no way we could avoid each other, so it was sort of a relief to get it over with. I wondered if he'd noticed Sam's arrival after he left me at the door the night of the picnic. And since he lived above me, I was almost sure he had.

I went over and spoke to him, although it was the last thing I wanted to do, and asked him if he'd let me see my aunt's portrait when he finished it.

"Why, sure, I'd be glad to," Kent said, then turned his back on me and squatted to scrub at a wire wheel, leaving me to stand there in silence. And he whistled. Just like the seven dwarfs, he whistled while he worked, but I was no Snow White and it stomped on my pride with a size-twelve boot. And to think I was feeling sorry for dumping him the way I did! You'd think the man could seem a little unhappy.

"By the way, I think you left your stereo on again," he called as I walked away.

Augusta hunched her shoulders, kicked up her feet, hips swaying in measured rhythm. She looked anything but angelic—until she glanced up and smiled. " 'Box Car Blues,' " she explained, stretching out a hand. "Here, kick off your shoes, there's plenty of room."

I hung back, or tried to. "Augusta, there's something I need to tell you."

It didn't do any good. I was placed firmly behind her. Now and again, she reached out to touch me, turn me in the right direction, until gradually something happened: I began to feel one with the music, and filled with the beat, my body moved in time. I closed my eyes and smiled. I could dance without even looking!

"You see," Augusta said. "It's fun."

"I wish you could help with the barn dance," I said, and told her about the proposed fund-raiser for

Summerwood. "We need somebody who can get people out on the floor, somebody who knows the dances."

"You have somebody," Augusta said, finally lighting on the sofa. "There's absolutely no reason why you can't do it yourself."

"But I don't know all those dances! I can't get up in front of all those people."

"Yes, you can. And you will if you want something badly enough." She locked in on me with her long, green gaze and I couldn't turn away.

"We'll see," I said. Maybe. Well, why not?

"Has anybody called?" I glanced at my telephone answering machine, which stared back with its red unblinking eye.

"Not since you left," Augusta said. "Whom were you expecting?"

"Somebody might have found Hairy," I told her. "And I thought I might hear from Sam."

Augusta thoughtfully swung one gold sandal on the end of her elegant toe and raised an eyebrow. "*Sam* probably went to church."

"My day wasn't exactly wasted," I said, showing off my Red Cross badge of courage. I searched the refrigerator for sandwich makings. "It looks like Bonita Moody was run down deliberately and they've found the car that did it."

She leaned over my shoulder, scooped vegetables from the crisper. "Really? Just the car? Who was driving?"

"That's what I was going to tell you. They're not sure. The owner's been in Maine for several weeks and somebody's been using it while she was gone. And Augusta . . . I think it's the same car that followed us that day we drove to Hughes."

"I thought you said that was Todd?"

"It did took like his car, but now I'm not so sure. This was a Cougar. Same color, and they look something alike."

I watched her concoct a salad that would do justice to the cover of *Gourmet*. Nosegays of radishes, frivolous spirals of carrot, a sprinkling of sprouts, three kinds of lettuce . . . and was that hearts of palm? Where did all this come from?

With Aunt Caroline's old wire whip, Augusta blended a tangy dressing with an onion-orange smell, then took two large bowls from the cabinet. "You can set the table," she said, lifting a warm, crusty loaf from the oven.

I put my mayonnaise and sliced turkey back in the refrigerator and did as I was told. "From now on, you're welcome to do the cooking," I said.

After we ate, Augusta sat serenely across the table for a few minutes without speaking, only to tell the truth, her eyes didn't took so serene. "Mary George, this isn't good," she said. "I'm afraid we're getting close to the truth."

"Isn't that what we want?"

"Yes, but not at the risk of someone's life. It certainly sounds as if somebody tried to kill Bonita Moody because of what they think she saw, and all because of the missing Bible. Your aunt realized its importance and put it away somewhere. I'm almost certain that was why she died." Augusta swished the dishes in the sink and waved them sparkling dry. "We have to find that Bible before anyone else gets hurt. Before you get hurt."

"I don't know where else to look," I said. "It wasn't anywhere in her house, and I certainly don't have it here."

"Then she must have hidden it somewhere else, in which case she probably left a clue."

"I don't think she had time. After all, Aunt Caroline didn't expect to die when she did."

"Nevertheless, there's that chance." Augusta leaned against the sink and folded her arms. "Now *think,* Mary George. *Think.*"

"The cookie jar," I said. I kept coming back to the cookie jar. "It was sitting in the middle of the attic floor."

She nodded impatiently. "Did you get a chance to look inside?"

"No, but there wouldn't be room for a Bible in there. And then that lady bought it by mistake." I shoved back my chair and started looking through the phone book. "Now, what was that woman's name again? Surely she's back from Europe by now."

There were two of them—cousins—and I had jotted the woman's name and number on the back of something, something that had been handy when I called before. And I had telephoned from my bedroom. In the second drawer of the bedside table I found one of those scented advertisements for perfume with a phone number and the name *Lottie Greeson* scribbled across the front. Hadn't she told Delia her cousin was due back this week?

She picked up on the fourth ring, sounding sort of breathless. "Sorry . . . we were eating watermelon out in the backyard." Lottie Greeson stopped to catch her breath and laughed. "My goodness, you'd think I'd run three times round the block!"

I told her who I was and reminded her about the cookie jar. "I believe you said your cousin bought it at the yard sale. Has she returned from her trip yet?"

142

"Edith? Oh, Lord, yes, honey! Got back early yesterday. Bless your heart, I plumb forgot to tell her about that, and they've gone over to Aunt Ella's in Mooresville for the afternoon. She turned ninety last week, you know."

I said I didn't know and sent belated good wishes. "When do you think I might get in touch with Edith?" I asked.

"If I have sense enough to remember, I'll phone her tonight," Lottie said. "But if you haven't heard by tomorrow, you might better give her a call. It's Lloyd Shugart on Campbell Road. You'll find it in the phone book."

"She sounds like a reasonable person," I said to Augusta as I came back into the living room. "Let's hope Cousin Edith's as laidback as Lottie."

But Augusta didn't seem to hear me. She stood in front of the sofa staring at the television with an expression of disbelief. "Tell me I'm not hearing this!" Augusta covered her ears. "Imagine talking about such things right in the family parlor. Where's that gadget that turns this thing off?"

I found the remote control and flicked off the commercial for a feminine hygiene product. Augusta sounded so much like Aunt Caroline I wanted to hug her. I guess I must have been smiling.

"What is it? What's so funny?" Augusta's face was flushed, her eyes flashed. "I don't know how things can change so much in fifty years, honestly I don't! Why, poor old Lucille Pettigrew would've had palpitations for sure if she'd seen something like that." And she patted her ample chest and sighed.

The next thing I knew, Augusta stood in front of the mirror adjusting a pert hat atop her pouf of hair. It was a

143

natural straw with bright green and turquoise streamers and a slightly turned-up brim, and Augusta looked like she'd just stepped out of a painting. She tweaked the hat this way and that, tilted it on her head, and posed, no doubt liking what she saw.

"Looks nice," I said. "Where'd you find it?"

"Can you believe somebody was throwing this out?" she said. "All it needed was a little fixing up. Now, where is my handbag?"

Augusta carries this bottomless tapestry bag that can produce anything from a toothbrush to a pair of hedge clippers. "Why?" I asked. "Are you going somewhere?"

"Somebody needs to keep an eye on Bonita Moody," she said. "Since she can't took after herself." She found her lumpy bag and opened it, and after poking about inside, seemed satisfied.

"When will you be back?" I asked.

"When it's time." She gave the hat a final poke, the bag a settling shake and headed for the door. "Don't worry, you won't be alone for long."

"How do you know?"

Augusta cocked her head and looked at me before she stepped outside. "Trust me," she said, and was gone. I ran to the door to look for her, but of course she wasn't there.

It wasn't fifteen minutes before somebody knocked at my door, and I opened it to find Sam Maguire standing on my step with a white paper bag in his hand. "Started to call you, and then I thought how disappointed I'd be if you weren't home, so I just took the chance and came anyway." He held up the bag and shook it. "Hope you like submarine sandwiches. Thought we might go on a picnic. I know a secret place."

I smiled. "You don't suppose we'll see clopadopalous

144

tracks?"

"Wouldn't be surprised," Sam said, and shook his head. "I can't believe you remember that."

"I can remember it. I just can't spell it," I said.

The brown stream still wound through the meadow, now dotted with cedars and pines, but Sam knew his way around, stopping only to pick a bouquet of daisies and Queen Anne's lace, which we stuck in an empty can on our picnic table. The table was our own big rock in a shady spot beside the water, only the rock didn't seem as big anymore.

Sam and I ate our sandwiches slowly and sipped slightly warm root beer we'd bought at a country store. He told me about growing up in Texas and working his way through a small college there. "I wrote to you when I left here," he told me. "Wrote you several times. Made me mad as all get-out when you didn't write back."

"I never got them," I said.

"I know. Dad admitted later he'd never mailed them. Didn't want me to have any connection with Summerwood. He hated having to leave me here. Guess he thought he could just erase it from my mind." Sam swirled the brown liquid in his soft drink bottle. "It didn't work that way."

"I'm glad." The rock was smooth and warm. I ran a finger along a crevice, trailed it in the cool water. "Somehow I thought you'd be married by now, raising a bunch of kids."

He laughed. "I am raising a bunch. That's what teaching amounts to, like it or not. I happen to like it. I was engaged for a few months right out of college, but both of us had second thoughts. Guess we just weren't ready. She went on to law school, and I got a job

145

teaching eighth grade science and went back to school for my masters."

*And what have you done with your life, Mary George?* I waited for him to ask, but he didn't. I hated to admit I'd dropped out after two years of college. If he ever did ask, I would just have to say I planned on going back in the fall. And now maybe I would.

Lying back on the rock, I listened to the sweet rush of water and watched late afternoon sunlight flicker through the leaves. I felt safe here in this good place with this good man, but all wasn't safe and good. I told Sam what happened to Bonita Moody and why.

"What makes you think that won't happen to you?" he said. "Mary G., why don't you go and stay with Delia, at least for a little while?"

"And what could Delia do? Anyway, I'm hoping to know more tomorrow." I told him about Edith Shugart and Aunt Caroline's cookie jar. "At least it's some kind of lead."

"How many people knew where this guy's aunt Alma kept her car? That she'd be away for a month?" Sam wanted to know.

"Let's see now . . . how many people are living in Troublesome Creek? Three or four thousand at least. Ours is a little town, Sam. Everybody knows everything."

"But they wouldn't know about the extra car key."

"No, I guess not," I admitted.

"Look, this is the worst possible time for me to have to leave, but I promised Ed this fishing trip a year ago, and this week's about the only time we can get together." He smiled. "At least it's only for a few days—or until my little brother gets enough of roughing it. You will be careful, won't you, Mary G.? I don't

146

want anything happening to you." Sam stood and took my hands, drew me up and kissed me, and the part of me that had been missing for so long was back where it belonged. And if we had been standing in water, we might've been electrocuted right there on the spot.

We stopped to see the Cummings at Summerwood on the way back, and since Rose offered dessert, Sam and I ended up staying longer than we'd meant. It's just about impossible for me to turn down homemade peach cobbler.

The answering machine blinked at me when I got home that night and I practically broke my neck in my rush to push the play button, hoping to hear someone had found my Hairy.

Instead it was the next best thing. "I think I have the cookie jar you're looking for," a woman's voice said. "It's packed away in my back storage room with some other things, and it's a little late to took for it tonight, but I'll try to get to it tomorrow. I'll give you a call when I find it."

Edith Shugart sounded sweeter than an angel. Well, almost.

# CHAPTER 18

BONITA MOODY STILL HADN'T REGAINED consciousness, I learned the next morning, but a hospital spokesperson said she was stable. I thought about her haggard husband sitting up with her all this time and hoped he was stable too.

"Mae Higgins said the Moody woman seemed a lot stronger this morning when she went off duty," Doc Nichols reported. His neighbor was a nurse on Bonita's floor, and he'd seen her having coffee in the Doughnut Barn. I wondered if Augusta had anything to do with the woman's improvement.

Word had gotten out about Walter Hildebrand's aunt Alma's car. It was being checked for fingerprints and other possible evidence, but so far I hadn't heard of any suspects. Now that Todd was more or less out of the picture, I didn't have any either. And that was even scarier.

Being a Monday, we had wall-to-wall patients, but as soon as there was a lull I checked my answering machine and heard that Edith Shugart had found my aunt's cookie jar. I could pick it up whenever it was convenient, she said.

I looked at the clock. It was convenient for me right now, but unfortunately we still had a couple of cats and a pregnant poodle to see before lunch.

When the phone rang at a little after one I was almost out the door. Doc Nichols had left a few minutes earlier and I started not to answer the call. It was probably Luanne Whitworth calling *again* from her mother's in Knoxville to check on that rotten Claudette. Luanne boarded her Maltese with us whenever she went out of town, then drove everybody nuts calling to see if we were following her instructions.

Still, it might be an emergency. Somebody's pet might suffer or die just because I was in a hurry. I groaned and went back to see who it was. After all, the cookie jar wasn't going anywhere.

The woman on the other end of the line asked for me by name, which is kind of unusual because I don't get many personal calls at the clinic. She was calling from the microchip company, she said. I recognized the system as the one Doc Nichols used to identify pets and hope flared like a tiny candle. Maybe . . . maybe . . .

"I think I might have some good news," she said. "We just got a call from an animal shelter in Gastonia, and it looks like they have your dog."

"Hairy! They've found Hairy Brown? When?" And to think I almost didn't answer the phone.

"Fellow brought him in yesterday. Said he was wandering around his neighborhood. They say he looks like somebody's been feeding him. Seems to have lost his collar, but his ID number checks out on the scanner. It's your dog all right.

"You might want to give them a call," she added. "Let them know the dog belongs to you. When do you think you'll be able to pick him up?"

"What about right now?" I said.

I put in a quick call to Doc's sister who agreed to fill in for me in case I was late getting back, and was on my way a few minutes later. If I didn't hit any traffic snags I should be there in less than an hour—but how on earth did Hairy Brown end up in Gastonia?

Hairy was dirtier, shaggier, and a little thinner, but he looked wonderful to me. He braced his big old feet against my chest and licked my face, and I hugged his smelly neck and cried. He rode home on the backseat with all the windows open, and as soon as we got back to the clinic, wolfed down a double portion of Canine Crunchies. After Doc checked Hairy over and pronounced him fit, I turned him over to the guy who does our grooming and told him to give him the works—which is more than I've ever been able to afford for myself.

"How do you suppose he got way over there?" I asked the doc.

"Who knows? Probably ran out when somebody

opened your door. Looks like he's been wandering around a good bit, but he could've gotten a ride. I expect somebody befriended him for a while."

For whoever did, I was grateful. On the way home I stopped at Anderson's Market for Hairy's favorite dog food, then stood in the kitchen watching him gulp it down. Augusta had left me a loaf of her wonderful bread, and I had several slices with a couple of bowls of soup. I realized now why I was so hungry. I had completely forgotten about lunch. I had also forgotten to collect the cookie jar from Edith Shugart.

I waited a little while to call her so I wouldn't interrupt her dinner. The two cousins had been so decent about letting me buy back the jar, I hated making a nuisance of myself, but Edith didn't seem to mind. "Why, of course, come right over," she said. "We were just sitting here watching one of those old game shows on TV."

The Shugarts lived a couple of miles out of town on Campbell Road and it took a few minutes to get there. Hairy sat behind me, his cold nose nudging my neck as I drove. I was glad to have him with me, not only for his company but because I was having that feeling again, that sensation of being followed. Lightning bugs winked in the gray dusk, and cars were beginning to turn on their lights, but you could still see to drive without them.

We passed a cornfield, dark green and shoulder high, a country church, gray in the fading light and circled by a low stone wall, then a pine thicket and the turnoff to the narrow side road where the Shugarts lived. I turned, then slowed and glanced behind me. A car passed, then another, bright headlights shoving back the night. The third car was dark and I was too far away to make out

150

anything but a vague shape. The driver seemed to hesitate at the entrance to the road, but obviously thought better of it and drove on. Probably somebody looking for a street, I decided, feeling slightly relieved. But not entirely. There were only three houses on Campbell Road. If someone had followed me, they wouldn't have to be Christopher Columbus to discover where I went.

A light burned on the porch of the Shugarts' neat white farmhouse, and Edith greeted me at the door. She looked to be in her midfifties and wore shorts, sandals, and a pink-smeared T-shirt. The whole house smelled sweetly of peaches.

"Come in, sit down a minute. Would you like some tea?" Edith ushered me past the dim living room where a television blared to the brightly lit kitchen. "Excuse the way I look. Been putting up peaches all afternoon, and I'm just too blamed tired to change."

I declined the drink, explaining that my dog was in the car, but sat at the kitchen table while she went to the back porch and returned with a box. It was the same box Aunt Caroline's coffeemaker had come in, the one that had held the cookie jar.

"I reckon this is all right," Edith said, pulling open the top to look inside. "To tell the truth, I haven't really looked at it since I brought it home. My sister collects cookie jars and this one looked so cute I thought she'd get a kick out of it, but another one will come along."

She started to remove the tissue, lift the ceramic dog from the box, but I reached out to stop her. "That's all right, you don't need to do that. I can see it's the one— see the chip on the ear? I did that when I was a little girl." I patted the smooth earthenware head. It would be good to have him back again—clue, or no clue.

151

Edith had paid three dollars for the cookie jar, and only asked for the same. I forced a five-dollar bill into her hand and practically ran to the car, refusing change. Still, she chased after me, protesting, across the yard. I think she would've hounded me all the way back to town if she'd had on good running shoes and hadn't been so tired.

I could hardly drive for curiosity about what might be in the jar, but I was afraid to stop and look inside. I didn't notice a car waiting when I left the Shugarts' street, but that didn't mean I wasn't being followed. At least I knew it wasn't Aunt Alma's gray Cougar. The police had impounded that.

By the time I got back to town I just couldn't stand it any longer. I had to cross Snapfinger Road to reach my place at Miss Fronie's, and on impulse I turned and drove the couple of blocks to Delia's, trying not to look at the still-empty house across the street. We hadn't had our formal closing so they hadn't begun renovations, and the old place looked forlorn and sad.

I parked in the back and let Hairy out on his leash for a minute before letting Delia know I was there. Naturally, Hairy wanted to come inside too, but Delia's cats didn't care for that idea at all, so we compromised. I left Hairy on the back screen porch where he settled for a snooze, tail thumping in contentment on the cool wooden floor.

"Oh, Lord!" Delia sighed when she saw what was in the box. "How many times have I seen Caroline fill that jar with cookies?"

"And how many times have you seen me empty it?" I said.

We opened the box on Delia's mahogany Chippendale dining table, now cluttered with half-filled packing boxes. "I won't be going to that stiff-necked condo," she explained, "but I sure don't plan to stay here and flutter around like some dusty old moth!"

"Uh-huh," I said. I had come up with what I thought was a brilliant idea for Delia's future and had mentioned it to Sam, but we weren't yet sure if we could work things out, so I kept my mouth shut for now.

I lifted the jar from the box and set the lid aside. There was something in the bottom of the jar. At first I thought it was merely a wad of tissue, but on touching it, I realized it was cloth.

Delia pushed up her glasses. "What is it, a rag?"

"Some doodad trimmed in lace. Looks like one of Aunt Caroline's hankies, and there's something inside." Carefully I unwrapped the small object and held it for Delia to see. "It's some kind of key, but I've never seen it. What do you suppose it opens?"

Delia picked up the key and examined it, adjusting her bifocals. "See that number on the back? Two-eight-four? That's either a locker at the airport or the bus station or the number of a post office box."

Since Troublesome Creek doesn't have an airport, and my aunt Caroline wouldn't go inside the local bus station unless a cleaning crew and an exterminating company went before her, the key had to be for a post office box.

I stuck the key deep inside the pocket of my shorts, gathered up the cookie jar, box and all, and woke my sleeping mongrel. Delia followed me outside. "Well?" she said as I urged Hairy into the backseat.

"Well, what?"

"What are you going to do now?"

"I'm going to the post office. Why wait?"

Delia moved down a step. "Mary George, do you

realize what time it is?"

I didn't, but she was going to tell me.

And she did. "It's after ten—probably closer to eleven, and you'll be going in there alone for anybody to see."

"Delia, it's right in the middle of town. There are lights."

"My point exactly. Somebody wants whatever's in there in a bad way. What's to keep them from following you there, watching you open that box? Do you think they would hesitate to take it from you any way they could? The post office is usually deserted this late. There wouldn't be a soul to stop them."

"You're scaring me," I said. "Stop it."

"Good. Now, promise you'll go straight home. Whatever's in that post office box will be there tomorrow. It's not going anywhere."

"Uh-huh," I said, and waved as I drove away. Surely Delia couldn't be serious. Now that I was this close, I meant to find out what was in that box and why it was so important. And I meant to do it tonight. After all, according to Sam, night is just day painted over. Isn't it?

But that was before I saw somebody watching from across the street.

# CHAPTER 19

THIS TIME A CHICKEN RODE HOME ON MY SHOULDER, and I bypassed the post office without hesitation. I was raised on Snapfinger Road. I know what should and shouldn't be there, and that dark, person-size shape standing just beyond reach of the streetlight shouldn't have been there at all. I spotted it by the stone wall on

154

the corner just before turning out of Delia's drive, and paused to see if it was somebody walking a dog, stopping to cross the street, but The Blob didn't move. It was waiting me out.

And Delia was right. The post office was brightly lit, but I didn't see a car in the parking lot. My neighbor had a point. Whatever was in that post office box would wait until tomorrow.

But the next day . . . well, if I were superstitious I'd say it was cursed.

In the first place, I was late leaving for work. When I had reached home the night before, Fronie was rehearsing for the international yodeling competition, or so it sounded. Whatever it was went on and on, and was much worse than awful. I made a decision right then and there to stay away from church that Sunday.

Then, just as I was about to drop off to sleep, Sam called from Atlanta and we talked for twenty minutes or more. He and his brother planned to leave early the next morning for a lakeside camp—far from telephones and civilization, he told me, and it would be several days before he called again. I told Sam about finding the key in the cookie jar, but not about being followed. After all, I wasn't *sure* I was being followed, and I didn't want him to know how nervous—oh, well, let's face it, neurotic—I'd become.

Of course it's difficult to hide something as obvious as that. "Mary G.," he said, "I really think you should wait on this. Why not let Doc Nichols keep that key, at least until I get back? You can trust him, can't you? It might not mean a thing, but if it does, just having it could put you in danger."

"Are you crazy? You want me to *wait* until you've caught your quota of fish? No offense, Sam, and I do

155

appreciate your concern, but there's no way I'm going to put off opening that box!"

"There's no use arguing with you, Mary G.," he grumbled. "But please be careful, will you? You know you're ruining my fishing trip. I won't be able to relax a minute for worrying about you."

I think I promised something ridiculous—that I would open the box at high noon in the company of an armed guard, or something crazy like that—but it got him off my back.

I was almost fifteen minutes late when I pulled into my usual space in the clinic's parking lot the next morning. I grabbed my purse with one hand and smoothed my hair with the other, hoping I'd get a chance to put on a little makeup later if we didn't have a heavy patient load that day.

He stepped in front of me so fast I almost ran smack into him, and for a minute I was so startled I couldn't speak.

Todd Burkholder took me by the shoulders and held them in a tight, uncomfortable grip. "Hey, just a minute! Don't be in such a hurry," he said.

"Get out of my way, Todd! You know you aren't supposed to be here, and I won't think twice about calling the police."

"Oh, don't I just know it." He gave me a slight shake, but his fingers relaxed on my arm. "This is a public parking lot, you little bitch. I have as much right to be here as anybody."

We shared the lot with a couple of dentists and the town's one florist, and as if in explanation, Todd waved a sickly-looking lily in my face.

"Get your hands off me *right now*," I said in somebody else's voice. I sounded meaner than a vegetarian at a barbecue. Good.

And it must have worked, because he did. Todd shook that pathetic flower in my face until the stem broke. "I've had it with you, Mary George Murphy! Because of you I'm probably going to lose my job—and for what? I didn't do a damn thing to you! Didn't follow you out to God knows where, and I sure as hell never broke in and searched your apartment."

Todd's face was an interesting shade of watermelon red. It reminded me of one of those new crayon colors. And he spit so when he talked I held up my purse like a shield. "Lady, you don't have a thing I want!" he said. (Well, that's not quite all he said, but I'll leave out the adjectives. Thank goodness Augusta wasn't listening!) After an apopletic pause, Todd hurled the lily in my direction, only it broke in two and flopped to the pavement.

Now he backed away from me, still sputtering. "All I wanted was a chance to explain. Now everybody thinks I'm some kind of pervert."

I never thought I would feel sorry for this jerk, and I still didn't, but I didn't plan to destroy his shabby little life. What this man lacked in manners and diplomacy, he made up for in sheer boorishness. What in the world made me think I was in love with this creep? No wonder Aunt Caroline flinched at his name!

"I guess I did accuse you unfairly," I said. "But you scared me half to death. If you want to discuss something, Todd, you don't lurk in the shadows and pounce. It tends to put one on the defensive.

"Look, if it will help, I'll call your boss and explain," I said.

If he'd had a cross, I think he would have held it in front of him. "Just stay away!" Todd screamed. "For

God's sake, stay away from me, woman!"

"Well, sure," I said, watching him leap into his car and scratch off. I jumped to get out of the way. One wheel backed over the lily. I didn't think I'd be seeing Todd again.

"I thought he was going to run over my toe," I told Doc Nichols later that morning as we shared some of his wife's oatmeal raisin muffins with our coffee. I could laugh about it now, although still somewhat shakily.

"That reminds me of what happened when I was trying to teach my son to drive," he said. "He'd practice backing down the driveway—up and down, up and down, and half the time he'd sideswipe his mama's pansy bed. Finally I got out of the car and stood in the yard to try and guide him past the trouble spot." Doc Nichols laughed. "And darned if he didn't run right over my toe! Couldn't walk for a week."

"You must have been a patient dad. I had to learn in driver's ed. Aunt Caroline didn't drive, you know."

"I know." The doc refilled his cup. "That was a sad thing, that accident. They say it was months before she'd even ride in a car."

"She wouldn't talk about it," I said. "I never knew exactly what happened."

"Car stalled on the railroad tracks. She barely escaped with her life." He frowned into his cup. "I was about ten or eleven at the time, but I'll never forget when it happened. Junior Witherspoon was in my class at school."

"Junior Witherspoon?"

"The boy who died in the accident. Well, his name was Albert, but everybody called him Junior. He was Delia Sims's little brother."

158

I guess he noticed my face, how I clutched the doorframe for support. "My God, Sport, I thought you knew that much!"

I shook my head. "Tell me about it," I said.

"There's really not that much more to tell. Caroline was about seventeen, maybe eighteen, and hadn't been driving long. Happened just before Christmas. She and Delia had been in town doing a little shopping, and of course Junior had to come along. I don't remember all the details, but it seems the other two were ready to leave before Delia, so she told them to go on without her, she'd walk home when she finished. It's not that far, you know."

Doc set down his mug and looked at me. "You sure you want to hear this, Sport?" I nodded. I had to hear it now.

"There was no signal at the crossing, and Caroline didn't see the train. She'd started across when she heard it, and I guess she panicked when the car stalled. She tried to get Junior to jump, but he froze. The people in the car behind them saw what happened. They said Caroline ran screaming to the passenger side, tried to open the door. They snatched her away just before the train hit."

I had heard Delia mention a brother who died, but I never knew how. Neither she nor my aunt ever discussed the accident in front of me. Everyone sort of tiptoed around the subject—it was something that happened long ago, and because of it, Aunt Caroline never drove. It was just one of my aunt's peculiar little quirks, and I never thought it was important. Until now.

Poor Aunt Caroline! What an awful thing to have to live with. And poor Delia. Once in a while I had noticed, or rather, suspected, a strained moment between the two friends, but then nobody's compatible 100 percent of the time. Now I wondered if the resentment went deeper, festered, until . . .

*Enough of that! This is Delia you're thinking about, Mary George Murphy.* I could never suspect our neighbor of hurting her best friend. But then I never thought Aunt Caroline would end up at the bottom of the back stairs with her neck snapped.

We had a couple of emergencies during our regular lunch hour that day, so I didn't get a break until later in the afternoon. As soon as I got a chance, I gave Delia a call.

She sounded pleased, welcoming, and that made me feel even more of a heel. "Mary George! You haven't opened that post office box, have you?"

"Not yet. Listen, is it okay if I come by for a minute after work? There's something I need to ask you."

"Well, of course, silly. I'd invite you to stay for supper, but I've been asked to fill in at bridge." She didn't even sound curious. "If I'm in the shower when you get here, just come on in. I'll leave the back door unlocked."

I drove straight to Delia's as soon as I could get away. Hairy would be wanting his supper and needing to go out, but surely a few minutes more wouldn't hurt. I had to hear about that accident from Delia herself.

No one answered when I knocked on the back door, so I opened it and stuck my head inside. "Delia?" I called, but there was still no reply.

"Delia, it's me, Mary George!" In the kitchen four cats cried at my feet and tried to trick me into feeding them again, but I knew my neighbor had already given her "babies" their dinner. I scooped up the big orange

160

tabby and walked into the living room to wait. Down the hall I heard the steady droning of the shower and hoped Delia wouldn't be long.

I glanced through an antiques magazine, read some recipes in *Southern Living,* and when the phone rang in the kitchen it jolted me from my communion with deep-dish chocolate delight. Thinking it might be Delia's bridge hostess calling about a change of plans, I was on my way to get it when the answering machine clicked on.

*"Delia, it looks like things are going to work out! It wouldn't do for you know who to find out about this, so the less said, the better. Remember, this is just between the two of us. I'll be in touch soon."*

I dropped the cat and hurried out the door, closing it quietly behind me.

The caller was Sam Maguire.

Why in the world was Sam calling Delia? And, supposing I was the "you know who" he was referring to, (and who else?) just what was it I shouldn't find out? I had mentioned to Sam that I thought Delia would make a perfect bookkeeper for Summerwood if we could arrange for her to live on the grounds, but we needed to refine the plan before presenting it to her. I wouldn't want to disappoint Delia if it didn't work out. No, it couldn't be that.

Sam had made it obvious he wouldn't be able to reach a phone from his "remote" camping area, yet here he was calling my neighbor when he should've been frying fish over his supper campfire. *There must be a reasonable explanation,* the rational side of me whispered calmly. But the doubting part of me shoved her roughly aside, sneering: *Are all men incapable of*

161

*telling the truth?*

And both Delia and Sam were determined, it seemed, to keep me from opening that box. Why?

Once home I clamped the leash to Hairy's collar and gave it a little jerk as I started for town. After all, Hairy was male too, and hadn't he run off to God knows where the minute the door was left open?

"Mary George! Wait up, what's your hurry?" I'd heard footsteps behind me, but was so wrapped in my thoughts I didn't pay much attention. Now I stopped to look back.

Breathing a little faster than usual, Kent caught up with me. "You look kind of flustered," he said. "You all right, Mary George?"

I'd have to feel better to die, I thought, but I didn't say so. And it wouldn't be a bad idea to have company on my walk to the post office, although there was still plenty of daylight left and people waved as they passed. If Kent Coffey had wanted to do me harm, he'd had plenty of opportunities. Besides, he could hold the dog's leash while I went inside the building. He didn't have to know what was in the box.

"Is everything okay?" Kent repeated.

"I think I'll soon be able to sit up and take some light nourishment," I said.

"What?" Kent almost walked into a tree.

I laughed. "That's just something Aunt Caroline used to say," I explained, seeing his concern. "I was joking, Kent. I'm fine. Really."

*At least as far as I know.* I patted the small key in my pocket. Soon I was going to find out.

# CHAPTER 20

THE DAY, WHICH STARTED OUT SULTRY BUT SUNNY, had darkened with my mood, and now it looked as if it might rain before we could get to the post office and back. Hairy didn't care, he was just glad to be outside, and would have sniffed every tree and post along the way if I hadn't kept a firm hand on his leash. Kent and I walked almost at a run, leaving no time for conversation, and I was glad. I wasn't in the mood for casual chatter.

"Do you want to go inside?" I asked Kent when we reached the gray stone building on the corner, but he shook his head. "I just came along for the company," he said, and with exaggerated puffing and panting, leaned against the side of the building.

I laughed and handed over Hairy's leash before I went inside. Kent really was a good sport. Maybe I had kissed him off too soon. Hadn't he always been agreeable? Maybe too agreeable. I couldn't manage to break that fragile thread of doubt. "I'll just be a minute," I said, searching my pocket for the key. "Gotta pick up my mail."

Did he know why I was here? I'd like to think Kent's eagerness to accompany me was strictly because of my sparkling wit, keen intelligence, and remarkable beauty, but some pious puritan voice inside said "Get real!" It had to be something else. Maybe the man just wanted exercise.

I stepped inside the small, stifling lobby, and it didn't take long to see I was alone. The post office had been closed for over an hour and the inner doors were locked. With the key in my fist, I searched the boxes in the

163

niche at the far end of the room. Number 284 was one of the larger ones on the bottom row. The whole time I stooped there to open the box, I sensed an imminent threat and resisted an impulse to look over my shoulder. *Silly! Cut it out. You're doing this to yourself!* I thought. But my fingers fumbled with the lock until at last I drew out the brown-paper-wrapped package inside. I hadn't realized how my hands were shaking.

The parcel, about the size of a cigar box, was addressed to me in Aunt Caroline's familiar script, and seeing her handwriting again reminded me of the hurtful, empty place she left behind.

Treetops bobbed and whispered in the rising wind as I came outside, and warm air from the pavement rose around us like a sauna. Kent glanced at the package under my arm. "Starting your Christmas shopping early, or is it your birthday?"

"Neither." I took the leash and darted for home. A raindrop fell. Perfect timing. "Friend of mine in Charlotte finally returned my book. I let her read my anthology by Southern woman writers—thought she'd never get it back to me."

"Oh," Kent said. He looked bored. I kept my arm over the local postmark.

"Want me to carry that?" he asked when the package slipped a little.

I clutched the bundle tighter and smiled, breaking into a run. "Race you!" I said.

We were about two-thirds soaked by the time we got home. "Aren't you going to ask me in for a cup of hot something?" Kent wanted to know. "Okay," I said with little enthusiasm, but he didn't get the hint. "Just give me a minute and I'll let you in the front." But first I took Hairy in the back so I could towel him dry in the kitchen.

I hadn't had dinner and no cup of anything was going to be enough for me. I looked in my freezer. "I can offer veggies and pasta in a lemon dill sauce or macaroni and beef," I said to Kent, thumping my offerings on the counter. Maybe he'd go home.

He didn't. Kent Coffey made a face and shrugged. "I'll take the macaroni."

"Then go wash your hands." I waved him away. "Maybe I can find some soup to go with this."

As soon as I heard the bathroom sink running I shoved my aunt's package in the freezer and piled two bags of broccoli on top. By the time he returned I had our dinner in the microwave and had set two places at the table. "What took you so long?" I asked when he finally appeared in the kitchen. I knew very well what took him so long. He'd been poking about my living room, looking, no doubt for the mysterious package. I thought I knew now why Kent had followed me to the post office. He wanted whatever was in that package. The knowledge made me nervous, but I pretended innocence. It was safer that way.

Kent was quiet over dinner, and I don't think it was just because of the food. I had the feeling he wanted to tell me something, but didn't know how to go about it.

"Kent, is something on your mind?" I asked later as I rinsed tomato soup from the pan.

He sat at the table nursing a cup of coffee, turning the mug in slow circles. "Funny, I was about to ask you the same thing," he said.

"What do you mean?"

"I mean I know something's going on, and that you could get hurt. I like you, Mary George. I don't want to see anything happen to you."

165

"Is that a threat?" I squirted soap into the pan. I would squirt him too if he made a move in my direction.

"Just call it a warning." Kent Coffey pushed his empty mug aside and stood. "I think you should get away from this place—and the sooner the better. Get out of here, Mary George."

Soap bottle in hand, I watched him turn and walk out my back door. It was the second time that day a man had left me standing speechless. I didn't waste any time locking the door behind him.

It wasn't quite dark, but I went from window to window closing blinds, drawing curtains, shutting out whoever might be *out there*. Rain thudded on summer-baked soil and sprayed the windows, pine branches brushed the roof.

The package was as cold as a Popsicle when I took it from the freezer, then, with Hairy Brown curling on the floor beside me, tore it open behind my locked bedroom door.

I recognized the old Bible at once. The curling cover was the cheap black kind made to took like leather, and my grandfather's name, Douglas Kincaid Murphy, was printed in tarnished gold on the front. My hopes began to fizzle. Obviously the value of this Bible wasn't in its cost or appearance. I would have to look further than that.

I found the note from Aunt Caroline tucked just inside the cover, and it apparently was written in a rush because I could barely recognize the handwriting.

*Mary George,*
 Please note family tree in front of Bible. Seems you have a living relative after all—but probably not for long, so time is of the essence! An uncle

166

Ben (your father's uncle) now lives in Hunters' Oak where you were born. Saw a story about him in the Charlotte paper the other day. Seems he used to be quite an adventurer and was presumed dead at the time your parents were killed. (See enclosed article.) Anyway, he went on to make quite a lot of money in real estate, etc., never married, and has no heirs—yet! I recognized the family name and the town, put one and one together, and came up with a sizable amount.

Made a call to "Uncle Ben" and told him all about you, but naturally he wants to meet you, and also wants proof. Bring your birth certificate—you have a copy—and this Bible along, but hurry! The old fellow's probably close to ninety and getting more senile by the minute. Oh—housekeeper's a tyrant—name's Milford. Watch out for him!

Now, listen, my dear girl, be on your guard as I'm afraid you have competition. There have been just too many questions, and I don't feel completely at ease. Let's hope it's my imagination, but I'm renting this post office box for good measure, and if you're reading this, you've received the key. Do get in touch with this old gent as soon as you can, but I don't think it's a good idea to go there alone.

Always,
Aunt C.


According to the enclosed article, dated several weeks before, Benjamin Franklin Murphy had fallen in love with Western Europe while serving with the Special Forces during World War II. After the war he returned to the States and struck out on his own to earn his fortune out West in ranching, land, oil, and stock investments. The writer portrayed my great uncle as sort of an eccentric who loved travel, theater, and the finer things in life, but kept pretty much to himself except for a select circle of friends. The last thirty years of his life had been spent in France and Italy, where he owned luxurious homes, and during this time he had broken ties with family and home. Now, apparently in his dotage, Ben Murphy had come home to Hunters' Oak, North Carolina, to live his remaining years in the house where he'd been born, and was seeking legitimate heirs whom he felt might deserve financial help.

I wanted to jump up and down and holler. I could certainly use the money; it was the "deserving" part that stymied me. As I slowly refolded the article, another part of me came to life, a part that was buried so deep I hadn't even known it was there. I remembered the big, white house in Hunters' Oak where my grandmother had lived, remembered the peeling paint on the wide front porch, and a rag doll named Lucinda. Dressed in blue calico, the doll sat under the huge Christmas tree in the room with the bay window. My grandma Ola had made her for me the Christmas I was four, just before she died. Except for my recent dream, I hadn't thought of Grandma Ola or Lucinda in twenty years.

Somewhere outside a car door shut, and I probably wouldn't have noticed it if it hadn't been for Hairy Brown. The dog rose from the rug by my bed, ears alert, and padded to the window, a growl low in his throat. The rain had stopped, but water dripped from the eaves, making it difficult to hear. I switched off my lamp and tried to peep through the blinds.

Through the unpruned shrubbery that screened my

view I saw Kent's car parked closer than usual to the house, but that was all. The backyard was steeped in soggy silence, and I watched for a while from the window to see if anything moved, but all I saw was an occasional glimmer of a puddle in the light from Fronie's kitchen.

"Good boy," I said to Hairy. "It's probably just Kent coming back from the Hound Dog with his supper after that awful meal I gave him, but if you hear anything else, you let me know." I stroked him between the ears and turned on the light.

And that was when I noticed the red blinking light on my answering machine. Two blinks for two calls. Both were from Delia. I had been so eager to open Aunt Caroline's mysterious package I hadn't glanced at it when I got home.

"Where did you go?" Delia said in her first brief message. "Thought you were coming by. Call when you get home. If you don't reach me here, I'm at Phoebe Martin's. Talk to you later."

The second was more urgent. "Now I'm worried. Tell me you didn't open that box alone. Mary George, something's not right. You get back to me now, I mean it!"

She had a point. Something definitely wasn't right. She and Sam had cooked something up behind my back—at least I supposed it was Sam. And for the first time I began to wonder if I might have been mistaken. How did I know this man was the Sam Maguire I'd known at Summerwood? After all, I hadn't seen him in twenty years.

*Oh, don't be silly, Mary George! He looks the way Sam would look and knows the things Sam would know—even calls me Mary G.* It had to be Sam. Yet people change, do things, even commit crimes we'd never suspect them of doing: the ones whose neighbors were always reported as saying, "Why, he was such a pleasant fellow, kind to animals, and helped old ladies across the street. He wouldn't harm a soul!"

And what about Delia? I *knew* Delia Sims, had known her most of my life. Surely she wouldn't do anything to hurt my aunt or me. Delia had come to an intersection in her life and didn't know which direction to take. Like me. If somebody had steered her wrong, I was sure she *thought* she was doing the right thing. My neighbor was lonely and she looked on me as her friend. Now I had let her down.

I called her home and left a message, thankful she was still playing bridge at Phoebe's and I wouldn't have to explain. "Just called to let you know I'm fine," I said. "I'll get back to you tomorrow. Don't worry."

I couldn't tell her about the Bible. Not yet. Couldn't take the risk of anyone else finding out.

Hairy paced the room whining until I finally let him out. He did his business quickly and galloped back inside, but his uneasiness continued, and so did mine. I made a cup of tea and sat down again with the Bible. It gave me a sense of belonging just holding it, seeing my name on the family tree.

My great-grandparents, Sarah and George Murphy, had three sons: Douglas (my grandfather), Benjamin, and Horace. Benjamin never married and had no children—at least none that he was claiming. Horace married and had two offspring: Eleanor, who died in infancy, and Fain, who was killed in the Korean conflict. My grandparents, Ola and Douglas, had one son, also named George, who had only me. Unless one of them had a child "on the wrong side of the blanket,"

170

as my aunt used to say, I didn't know where my competition would come from.

I looked at the clock. Not quite ten. Would ancient Uncle Ben still be awake? I just couldn't wait until morning.

I called information, and then his number.

"Igor" answered. Igor with an English accent and a pronounced snarl, and from the sound of him he seemed to be having a really rotten day and wished for me the same. Ah! I thought. Milford, I presume?

Mr. Murphy didn't take calls after nine o'clock, I was told, and was getting ready to retire for the night.

And how is dear Uncle Ben? I wanted to say. Tell him to hang on awhile longer, I'll get there as fast as I can. But I didn't, of course. I told this snobby servant my name and how I was related to his employer. "I believe my aunt Caroline called several weeks ago."

"Yes. Quite a while back." He wasn't going anywhere with this, and obviously neither was I.

"I'd really like to meet him. You see, Aunt Caroline died last spring, and I was going through her things when I found our family Bible. My grandfather, Douglas, and your Mr. Murphy were brothers," I explained.

"I see."

"And when will it be convenient for me to come?"

Silence. Then a sigh that must have weighed a ton. "One moment please. I'll see."

He was gone a lot longer than a moment, and if Uncle Ben hadn't been so rich, I'd have hung up. But to be honest, I did want to meet the old coot—money or no money. He was the only living relative I had, or at least the only one I knew of.

"Mr. Murphy will receive you the day after

171

tomorrow, Milford informed me. "He has sherry at five and a light meal at five-thirty. If it's possible, he'd like for you to join him." I could tell by the servant's tone he wasn't exactly thrilled with the idea of my coming—and with good reason. If I inherited, he'd definitely be the first to go.

"I must ask you not to linger after dinner," he added in a growly whisper. "Mr. Murphy tires easily, and the excitement might keep him awake."

"Of course," I said, and smiled as I hung up the phone. To think that a man would lie awake because of my stimulating company gave my morale an unexpected boost, even if he was as old as Uncle Ben.

I was still smiling when Doc Nichols called to tell me Aunt Caroline's house was on fire.

# CHAPTER 21

I GOT THERE IN TIME TO SEE A BLACK TOWER OF SMOKE eddy and climb above the charred remains of what once was Uncle Henry's garage. A timber fell, sending dark ashes swirling in a gust of wind, and I jumped when a hand clutched my shoulder.

"Thank God they got to it before it reached the house!" Doc Nichols said behind me. "Fred Mabry told me if it hadn't been for the rain, it would've spread before they could stop it."

Fred Mabry was Troublesome Creek's fire chief who now stood to the side with his hose crew watching to see if the flames would leap up somewhere else, I didn't see how they could, the whole place was drenched in swamp-black water. Oily puddles, like tentacles, reached for our feet, and everyone stepped back—

everyone being the crowd of onlookers that seem to appear within five minutes of disaster. Every town has them, and ours is no different. There's Emma Norris down the street who always embroiders on even the most horrifying facts, and poor old Millie Satterfield, who cries. Millie cries not only at disasters but at football games, parades, graduations, and cats stuck in trees. And then there's Mr. Puckett, the butcher at Anderson's Market, who thinks everything's a communist plot. Delia says she just runs when she sees him and has about decided to become a vegetarian.

"Fire didn't start by itself," he announced, shoving his soot-smeared face into mine. "Looks like somebody tried to burn you out, little lady!"

I cringed, more at the "little lady" than at the Puckett Pronouncement, because this time he was right. It didn't take a bloodhound to detect the stinging smell of kerosene, and later Fred Mabry told me one of his men had found a shred of oil-soaked rag.

Arms grabbed me around the waist and somebody's hair tickled my chin. "Mary George, thank heavens you're all right!" Delia said, looking up at me in the glare of a gawker's headlight. "I didn't know where in the world you were. Came home and heard the sirens— dear God, it scared me half to death!" And she gave me another squeeze.

I put my arm around her, led her away through the thinning crowd. People were going home now that they realized the show was over. "I'm sorry. I left you a message . . . and I'm okay. It could've been a lot worse." My legs felt so shaky I had to stop a minute and hold on to the scaly old sycamore in the front yard. We were due to close on the house in a few days, and if that fire had spread, I wouldn't have had anything to close on. There was no telling how much it was going to cost to get the burned debris cleaned up.

"Mary George, why don't you stay with me tonight?" Delia said. "I hate to think of you being alone."

"I'll be okay as soon as I can get home and wash this smoke from my hair," I said. My clothes and everything were permeated in the dark, smothering smell. And frankly, I didn't want to wake the next morning and look out on the sad mess in my aunt's yard. "And don't forget, I have Hairy here." I tapped on the back window of my car where the big dog lay sleeping. I wasn't about to leave him at home with all this going on.

"Don't worry, I'll see her home," Doc Nichols said. "Sport, are you okay to drive?"

I nodded. "I'm fine. Really." Why was everybody treating me like an invalid? I was shaken, but I was also good and mad. Why would somebody do this to me? It didn't make sense. If somebody wanted to put me in danger, why set fire to an empty house on the other side of town?

Still, I was glad for the doc to follow me home, and he waited dutifully on my doorstep while I unlocked my front door. I didn't want to admit it, but I was relieved when he insisted on coming inside—to scare off any critters, he said.

"At least it won't take long," I told him, trying to make a joke. "After we check my one closet and look under the bed, there's no place for anybody to hide."

But the doc's face was grim when he stepped past me and looked about. "Looks like we're too late, Sport. I'm afraid your visitor has come and gone."

This time the searcher had been more careless. Cushions were upturned on the sofa, the drawer of the end table had been emptied on the floor, pots and pans littered the kitchen, cabinet doors swung open. I dreaded to look in the bedroom.

Dresser drawers and closet were all in disarray, sheets wadded and thrown to the floor, and my mattress had been pulled from the bed, but it didn't look like anything was missing.

Now I knew why somebody had set fire to Uncle Henry's garage. "Three guesses as to what they were looking for," I said.

Doc Nichols nodded. "Well, they didn't find it here."

And they wouldn't, because I had taken the family Bible along with me when I met the doc at Aunt Caroline's, and he'd locked it safely in the trunk of his car.

We tried not to touch anything while we waited for the police, but we did look around to see if we could find out how the intruder came in, and Doc found a broken window over the kitchen sink, and shards of glass were scattered on the ground below.

"Looks like somebody broke the glass, then reached inside to unlatch the window, and climbed in over the sink," I said. But the doc didn't answer. He only shook his head.

"Pack a bag, you're coming home with me," Doc said after Dennis Henderson and another policeman had come and gone. "We have plenty of room, and that's what guest rooms are for." He grinned. "Besides, it'll give Kate an excuse to make her blueberry waffles for breakfast."

"What about Hairy?" I asked.

"The beast comes too."

I didn't argue.

That night I dreamed about Augusta. It was funny, but

175

with all the weird things going on, I hadn't thought that much about her; I guess I didn't have time, but I did miss her company and wondered if Bonita Moody was going to pull through.

As if in answer to my thoughts, Ray Moody called me the next afternoon at work. His wife had regained consciousness, he said, and wanted to talk with me. I told him I'd come by the hospital as soon as I could get away, but she stayed on my mind the rest of the day. Did Bonita Moody know more than she was telling about the way Aunt Caroline died?

The police hadn't found any prints in my apartment other than those that would have been there anyway, and seemed to be thoroughly bamboozled. And so was I. From what Doc and I learned from our local spy sources, there weren't any unfamiliar prints on the car that hit Bonita either. Whoever was doing this had watched enough detective shows on television to know to wear gloves. Well, Aunt Caroline always said a little knowledge is a dangerous thing, and I just had to hope my intruder would eventually trip himself up.

Bonita was sleeping when I stopped by to see her after work, but the nurse insisted on waking her. It was time for her supper, she said. Since Ray had gone down to the cafeteria for a bite, I positioned the tray over Bonita's bed and cranked up the head so she could eat her chicken soup and disgusting green gelatin. I could tell she wasn't real excited about it, and who could blame her?

Bonita was still kind of groggy and didn't seem to remember me, so I wiped her face and hands with a damp cloth and that perked her up a little. I looked around for Augusta, but she must've gone on break too. Maybe the hospital cafeteria was featuring chocolate cake.

I waited until she'd finished most of her soup before I reminded her who I was. "Your husband said you wanted to see me," I said.

She looked blank.

"Mary George Murphy," I said. "My aunt Caroline—"

Bonita sipped water from a straw. "Oh, yes. Right. There was something—well, it might not mean anything—but the day I was there, the day your aunt died, I heard somebody in the house." She took my hand and squeezed it and was surprisingly strong, I thought, for somebody who had been in a coma. "Listen, I *know* they were there, I could feel it. And there was that sound, that soft, creaking kind of shuffling sound people make when they're trying to be quiet."

"Did you see anything?" I refilled her water glass.

"I saw a car. Black or dark blue, I think. It was parked out back, sort of hidden by a trellis. I didn't hang around to find out who it was."

"So you didn't actually see them?" I had been hoping for more than this.

"Just a shadow there at the end of the hall, then it sort of disappeared into the kitchen. It could have been anybody, but it definitely wasn't my imagination."

"Why didn't you say something about this before?" I'm afraid my impatience showed in my voice.

Her eyes sparked back at me. "For the very reason you see me in this hospital bed! I didn't want whoever was there to know that I'd seen them."

But somehow they had found out. And they still didn't know Bonita Moody hadn't gotten a look at their face. Before I left that day, I waited to tell Ray Moody what his wife had said. "If I were you, I warned him,

"I'd ask the police to put an extra guard by her door."

I had left Hairy with Doc's wife, Kate, that morning, and now stopped to collect him on my way home. I found him happily splashing in the wading pool with the children next door. Of course he didn't want to leave, so I had to lure him into the car with a doggie bone and a sugary voice. When I reached home I was tired and irritated and dreaded the prospect of cleaning up last night's topsy-turvy mess.

Kate Nichols had offered to come and give me a hand, but I was reluctant to share the bits and pieces of my personal life that had been scattered throughout my three small rooms.

The first thing I noticed was the front screen door. It was slightly ajar, and for a minute I froze in the middle of the walkway with my hand on Hairy's collar. I was sure I had pushed the screen shut when Doc and I left the night before. Damn! Had my vandalizing tormentor come back again?

At least now I knew who it wasn't. It wasn't Todd Burkholder. Dennis Henderson had called me at work to tell me Todd was in Richmond on a business trip and had spent last night at a hotel there. Maybe this would let him off the hook with his employer.

I found the package propped between the screen and the door. It was large and flat, wrapped in brown paper, with a message scribbled on the front in bold, black ink:

*Mary George,*
　　Here's the portrait of your aunt commissioned by her church. I hope you will deliver it for me and that it meets with their approval. Please remember what I said last

178

night, and follow my lead. Be careful, and good luck!

*Kent*

"Follow my lead?" What did he mean by that? And why didn't Kent deliver the portrait himself? I knew the police had questioned him about searching my apartment the night before, but as far as I knew nothing had come of it. Would Kent have had time to douse Uncle Henry's garage with kerosene and set fire to it after sharing my meager meal? Maybe, but I wasn't sure. And hadn't he tried to warn me? What was it he'd said? "Get out of this place," or something like that. Which meant that Kent Coffey knew something I didn't.

It also meant he had left, flown the coop, so to speak. When I went upstairs to check, I found his door unlocked and his few possessions gone.

# CHAPTER 22

PHYSICAL LABOR IS SUPPOSED TO BE A CALMING process. It wasn't. I picked up pots and pans, stacked them in my gaping cabinets, collected the strewn contents of dresser drawers, straightened a lampshade here, a sofa cushion there, and all the time I was thinking, *somebody is watching me, somebody is waiting. Waiting for me to lead them to the Bible.* They had killed for that Bible and I didn't think they would have any qualms about doing it again, only this time the victim would be me—Mary George Murphy!

Uncle Ben had asked me to bring the family Bible along as proof of our kinship, but a birth certificate would do as well, and I had a copy of mine. The person who killed Aunt Caroline hadn't meant for me to learn about my rich old uncle Ben who was just about to totter into the Everlasting Arms. But now that I had, there was only one solution. I had to be eliminated. Then the Bible, of course, would be destroyed. The stark reality of my predicament was not reassuring.

If anything happened to me, who would suspect that an Orphan Annie like Mary George Murphy might stand between my aunt's killer and Uncle Ben's fortune?

Delia would know about my family connections. And Sam—although I wasn't sure Sam believed me. And that wasn't all I wasn't sure of about Sam Maguire. He had dropped back into my life with his familiar Peter Pan enthusiasm, and now he was gone. Again. Where?

Doc Nichols knew about the family Bible, and with my permission had locked it in his safe deposit box at Troublesome Creek National Bank until I needed it for my meeting with Uncle Ben. The doc would create a great big stink if somebody did me in, I was sure of it. But would the killer care? I doubted it.

And then there was Kent. He had followed me to the post office and home again. Quite possibly, he had even set fire to the garage on Snapfinger Road so he could search my apartment . . . and then had the nerve to warn me before he disappeared. I flopped on the sofa and pulled Hairy's big head into my lap. Had Kent Coffey warned me against himself?

Kent Coffey. *Coffey*. When I made the connection, it blinked in my brain like a misspelled word on a computer screen, and I ran to the kitchen for Aunt Caroline's copy of *Troublesome Creek Cooks*. There it was, just where I'd left it on the shelf by the sink, only the page with the recipe was missing. I thumbed slowly, carefully through the book, shook the pages, but it just

180

wasn't there. Never mind. I remembered seeing the page my aunt had marked in the open cookbook in her kitchen, and it was turned to a *coffee* dessert!

Aunt Caroline hadn't had time to write a note, point a finger when the murderer appeared at her door. But somehow she'd managed to stall him in her kitchen long enough to leave a clue. I remembered now that Delia had questioned her plans to serve a fattening dessert when everyone was dieting.

When Fronie Temple appeared at my door a few minutes later I was almost glad to see her. At least she hadn't brought one of her inedible concoctions.

"Heard you had another visitor last night, and thought you might need a hand putting things straight. I feel just awful about this, Mary George. Wish there were something more I could do." My landlady stood in the doorway fingering her bright purple necklace and waited to be asked in. "Sorry to hear about that fire at your homeplace—don't hold your breath till they find out who did it. I swear, I think I could dig up every one of those azaleas in front of city hall and cart them off in a wheelbarrow in broad open daylight, and those lazy police wouldn't notice a thing!"

"Miss Fronie," I began, ushering her inside. "Tell me what you know about Kent Coffey."

"I know he's gone. Left in the middle of the night owing two months rent." She stood in my living room looking about, shaking her head. "And to think I trusted that young man, gave him the benefit of the doubt. Why, I even recommended him to paint your aunt Caroline's portrait for the choir room. Reckon he's gone off with that too."

She looked so old, so tired and forlorn that I went over and put my arms around her. I was going to tell her about the portrait when the phone rang in my bedroom.

"I hear that movie-star-looking fellow upstairs from you has given them the slip," Delia Sims said. "Bet you ten to one he set that fire, Mary George. After that box you got at the post office, I reckon." She paused. "Didn't find it, did he?"

"Don't worry, the Bible's safe," I whispered, glancing through the door at Fronie preening in the mirror over my living room sofa. "Look, I have lots to tell you, but I can't talk now. Why don't you ride with me over to Hunters' Oak tomorrow? I have a date with a rich uncle."

"You have a date with who? What are you talking about?"

"I still have a relative living in Hunters' Oak," I said. "My father's uncle, Benjamin Franklin Murphy. He's filthy rich, has no other kin, and is almost as old as that fruitcake you and Aunt Caroline used to pass back and forth every Christmas. *And* he's asked me to come for dinner tomorrow night. I'll call and ask if I can bring a friend."

"Oh, my goodness, Mary George! Do you suppose that's what all this is about? Caroline must've known, or at least suspected . . . Dear God! Caroline—my poor Caroline! Now I suppose whoever killed her will be after you!"

I made a face. I didn't need reminding. "After tomorrow, it will be too late, but I would like somebody to keep me company on the drive over. And frankly, I'm not sure how to get there. You will go with me, won't you?"

"Well, of course. If Uncle Ben's as rich as you say, he shouldn't mind an extra person for dinner. What time do you want to leave?"

"I've asked for half a day off, so why don't we plan on leaving around noon and stopping somewhere for lunch?"

"Suits me," Delia said. "But where are you staying tonight? Didn't you tell me they broke your kitchen window? Anyone could get in."

"Doc sent somebody over to replace that. I'll be fine right here, and Hairy's with me; I promise to lock up tight." With Kent Coffey out of the picture, I felt a little less threatened. If the man were to return, he'd have to face not only Hairy and me but a belligerent landlady as well. "I'll meet you here around noon," I said.

"Meanwhile, chew on this, Mary George," my neighbor said. "If your uncle doesn't have other heirs, who would inherit after you?"

Some distant relative I'd never heard of? A cutthroat "cause" of some kind? I couldn't imagine who would go to such lengths to eliminate the competition, and I certainly didn't want to meet up with them. But then, I reminded myself, probably I already had.

The more I thought about it, the more I convinced myself that Kent Coffey had murdered my aunt, set fire to Uncle Henry's garage, and, not finding what he was looking for in my apartment, fled before the police could investigate further.

"I hope you plan to notify the police about your missing tenant," I told Fronie, "because if you don't, I will. I think Kent Coffey is guilty of a lot more than running arrears in his rent."

"To tell you the truth, the thought did cross my mind," Fronie said. "After all, we never had any trouble like this before. But he seemed such a *sweet* young man, so thoughtful, don't you know? What on earth do you suppose came over him? Do you think he could be on

183

dope, or something like that?"

I said I didn't care what Kent Coffey was on as long as he was on his way far from here, but I did call my friend Pat Callaghan at the police station and pass along my suspicions and a description of Kent's car.

The next morning Pat phoned just as I was getting out of the shower to report that they hadn't yet found a trace of Kent or his car, but that Bonita Moody was being dismissed from the hospital and would be staying for a few weeks with a relative.

"Good—as long as it's not around here," I said, hoping she would be safe.

"Couldn't tell you if I knew, which I don't," Pat said. "But it's somewhere out of state, I think."

I wondered if Augusta had gone along as well, and was beginning to feel completely abandoned when Delia phoned to see if I'd survived the night.

"Oh, goody," she said when I answered. "I'd be most disappointed to learn you hadn't made it after you promised to buy my lunch today."

I laughed. "Then I hope you like barbecue. Doc told me about this great place near Albemarle if you can hold off that long."

"I'll be on your doorstep before noon," she said.

But she wasn't. When I reached home at a little after twelve that day I found a note on my door written on the back of an envelope.

Tried to call you at work, but line was busy.
Got a call from realtor—somebody from out of
town made an offer on my house and they want
to meet for lunch. Sorry—I hate this, but won't

be able to go with you. Call when you get back!

*Delia*

The phone was ringing as I let myself inside and I hurried to answer. I hadn't been aware that Delia had made a decision about selling her house. Maybe she'd changed her mind about going with me. I dreaded driving across the state alone, and I was terrified of meeting tyrannical Uncle Ben.

"Mary G.!" Sam said. "Boy, am I glad I caught you. They told me at the vet's you were on your way to— what's the name of that place again?"

"Hunters' Oak," I said. "And where are you? Didn't know they had telephones at Lake Catchacold—or wherever it is you went."

"The truth is, we didn't catch much of anything and I came back a day early. I'm at a gas station just on the other side of Charlotte . . . and do I detect maybe the faintest hint of resentment? What's the matter, Mary G.?"

"I was there when you left that message at Delia's," I said. Now, why did I tell him that?

"Oh. Well, damn, Mary G.! Now you've ruined it. Why didn't you say something?"

"Ruined what?" I looked at my watch. "Look, I've got to hurry. If I'm late, Uncle Ben might not leave me his millions."

"Ruined my surprise. Remember our buddy Cindy? Used to help in the kitchen at Summerwood? I've found her, Mary George. She's cooking at this resort in the north Georgia mountains—says they're all a bunch of old farts, and wants to get out. I think I may have talked her into coming to the camp, or at least giving it a try,

185

and she's going to stay with Delia until we can work something out . . ."

"Uncle Ben? What millions?" Sam did the backstep all over his tongue.

"I'll have to tell you later. I'm on my way to meet him right now, and it takes several hours to get there." But I just had to know. "How did you ever find Cindy?"

"Mr. Mac told me about her. Seems they kept in touch. And I was in the area anyway, so I stopped in for a visit. Told her about you . . . and that's not all, Mary G. I think we might be able to—"

"Sam, really, I've got to go."

"Okay. Look, I know where Hunters' Oak is. Why don't I meet you for lunch somewhere? We'll leave my car and ride together. That is, if you'd like the company."

I'd like the company very much and told him so. "Delia stood me up," I said, and told him about her note. "So I guess you'll have to do."

We agreed to meet at the barbecue restaurant in Albemarle. *If only it were closer!* I thought. I changed into a sea green sundress with full skirt and modest jacket I hoped would meet with my elderly uncle's approval, then fed Hairy and let him out for a quick run; Doc had promised to stop and check on him after work. I was on my way to the car when Fronie appeared as suddenly as if she'd been dreamed up by a genie with bad fashion sense.

She wore a polyester pants suit of a large floral design in neon pink, some sort of zebra-striped turbanlike head covering, and carried a picnic hamper the size of Alabama.

"Mary George, I hope this isn't an intrusion, but Delia told me she wasn't going to be able to ride over to

186

Hunters' Oak with you, and I wondered if you'd mind if I went along?" My landlady lifted the basket as she spoke. It looked heavy. Real heavy. "Thought you might like a little something to eat along the way. Made some of my poppyseed muffins fresh today."

*Right. And the ones you brought Aunt Caroline were stale!* I remembered. "I'm sorry, Miss Fronie," I said. "But I'm meeting a friend for lunch, and I really don't know how long I'll be. It might be late."

"That's all right, honey. I just want a ride to see some kinfolks over there. My first husband was from Hunters' Oak, you know, and I never get a chance to visit. They're always gettin' on to me about that."

Fronie swung the hamper onto the backseat and slammed the door. "Oh, well, I'll just bring this along. You never know when we might get hungry."

I stood speechless with my hand on the door handle. I didn't know what to say. I wanted to say, "Bug off, you frumpy old bag! Can't you see I want to be alone with my sweetie?" But Aunt Caroline's gentle ghost would haunt me.

Fronie was walking around to the passenger side when I saw the paper in my seat. What was the missing page from my aunt's cookbook doing on the seat of my car! I snatched it up and stuffed it into my handbag along with the old family Bible Doc had been guarding for me. I wasn't going to let that handbag out of my sight.

"Okay, let's go," I said as Fronie Temple plopped onto the seat beside me. "I told Sam I'd meet him in Albemarle in an hour, so we'll have to take the quickest route."

"Then you'd better take the Bethel Church Road. They're doing construction work on the expressway and

187

the right lane's closed for miles. Althea Jernigan said she just about wet her pants before she could get to a rest stop the other day." Fronie strained to get the seat belt around her bulging middle. I sighed and followed her directions, turning onto the two-lane road past Bethel Church. Did Fronie mean to spend the night with her relatives? I hoped so. At least Sam and I would be alone on the return trip. I had promised Doc I'd be at work in the morning, and I knew we'd be late getting home, but I didn't care.

And if I hadn't been aggravated with my landlady, I would have been in high spirits, although it had been a demanding morning. We'd seen one frantic pet owner after another until finally, about midmorning, there had been a brief lull. Doc had managed to grab a doughnut and a quick cup of coffee and was on his way to check on a post-op puppy when he stopped halfway across the room and looked at me.

"The glass." That was all he said, just "The glass."

I kind of smiled and shook my head. Doc works much too hard. "Yes?" I said.

"That broken window in your kitchen. If it had been broken from the outside, the glass would've been in your sink."

"What?" I stopped to answer the phone, and David Angel, the Baptist minister, came in just then with his pet ferret, and that was the end of that. Now it came back to me.

Beside me Fronie Temple leaned back, closed her eyes, and hummed, sounding sort of like a cat in the mood for more than holding hands. To discourage her, I turned on the car radio just in time to hear the end of the news.

"*. . . And this just in from Watauga County. The state*

*patrol has discovered a white Honda Civic with a North Carolina license plate that apparently went off the road in the mountains near Blowing Rock. The driver is still trapped inside. Rescue workers are attempting . . ."*

I glanced at Fronie but she didn't seem to have heard it.

Kent Coffey drove a white Honda Civic.

# CHAPTER 23

I LOOKED AT THE CLOCK ON THE DASHBOARD. "I'M afraid we're going to be late. How far is it to the turnoff?"

"A good little ways," Fronie said. "But I know a short cut just a few miles down the road. It comes out about the same place and doesn't wind around so much. Might save some time." She studied herself in the visor mirror and concentrated on centering her funny-looking hat. It looked as if it came straight from the forties.

Augusta had been on my mind all day and I wondered why. Usually I could sense when she might appear, catch a whiff of her strawberry scent, feel reassured by the awareness of her gentle presence, but Augusta wasn't near. Maybe she had accomplished her mission and moved on to someone who needed her more. But you'd think she'd at least wait to tell me good-bye.

And right now I could use some heavenly direction because I had a dismal feeling we were going the wrong way. "Okay, which way now?" I asked Fronie when we came to the next intersection.

She glanced in both directions. "Right . . . I think."

"You think? I thought you knew where we were going. We've been wandering around out here for an

189

hour. Sam's going to think I've stood him up."

But I turned right and drove for another mile or so until I saw the sign. "Miss Fronie, we're headed back toward Charlotte. This can't be right! We must be miles out of the way."

"I'm sorry, Mary George. Guess I told you wrong back there. We should've turned left. I sort of got turned around—just wait till you get to be my age, honey. Your mind goes on vacation and forgets to invite you along."

At this rate I'd probably get to be her age before we reached that barbecue place in Albemarle, I thought as I looked for a place to turn around. I would have to call the restaurant at the next available telephone and tell Sam we were on the way.

But the next available phone was at a gas station-general store about three barns, five cornfields, and fifteen miles down the road, and I had to wait another ten minutes for the woman who was using it to inquire about every one of her eleven grandchildren. I looked at my watch as the woman shifted her handbag and her feet. It was 1:36. If the small store was air-conditioned, it wasn't working today, and the ceiling fan over the produce stirred only hot air.

I watched flies buzzing around a box of peaches and felt a little weak in the stomach. The English muffin and apple juice I'd had for breakfast seemed like ancient history and I wiped the perspiration from my face with a tissue.

"Honey, your face is as red as those tomatoes," Fronie said. "For heaven's sake, go splash some water on it and get yourself a cold drink. Here—what's that number? I'll call that barbecue place." And she planted herself behind the long-winded grandmother, who gave her a withering look.

I really did have to go to the bathroom, and the idea of a cold drink overruled anything else, including my need to speak with Sam—who was probably sitting in an air-conditioned restaurant drinking iced tea. I gave my landlady my credit card and the name of the barbecue place and headed for the back of the store. Sam would wait for me. He would order his sandwich and eat it while waiting for me to join him . . . and then he would probably order another.

I felt refreshed after washing my face, and took a long gulp of icy Coke before seeking out Fronie. I found her fanning herself beside the car.

"Spoke with the cashier at that restaurant, Mary George. She said your young man's done left."

"What? Left for where?" This wasn't like Sam. "Are you sure? Did he leave a message?"

"Well, he did ask if you'd been there, she said. Maybe he called your place, left a message there."

Of course! That's what he would do. I drank the rest of my soft drink and went back inside to phone. Talking Grandma, thank goodness, had bought a basket of homegrown tomatoes and left. I called my apartment twice, thinking I must have dialed the wrong number, but the answering machine never picked up.

"Funny," I said to Fronie as we got underway, "I don't remember turning off my machine, but the phone just kept on ringing."

"I expect you just forgot." She patted my arm. "And don't worry, your Sam will understand." Fronie blotted a fresh layer of purple lipstick. "April Orchid," she called it, although I've never seen orchids that color in April or any other month.

Just then I didn't much care if Sam understood or not. I was a bit perturbed with Sam Maguire for leaving the

191

way he did. It wouldn't kill him to wait a little while longer. After all, how did he know I hadn't had a flat or something? It just wasn't like him.

And it wasn't like Delia, either, to go off to lunch with a stranger—even if he did want to buy her house—after seeming so eager to make the trip to Hunters' Oak. I knew she couldn't afford to pass up a house sale, but couldn't she have tried to reschedule the meeting?

If my aunt's old friend was as concerned for me as I thought she was, Delia Sims certainly wouldn't want me driving alone all the way to Hunters' Oak with the coveted family Bible in my handbag.

And a little doom-saying moth flitted inside my head, whispering, *Something's wrong . . . something's wrong . . .*

According to the map I had bought back at the store, we were a good half hour from Albemarle, and then it would take another twenty minutes or more to get on the interstate and head east toward Raleigh and Rocky Mount. With luck, and if a big rock didn't fall on me, we just might make Uncle Ben's by five as Igor had instructed.

The sun was bright and the asphalt road shimmered in the glare. My eyes ached. My head ached. There were too many thoughts in there. Too many doubts. What was that Doc had said? If somebody had broken into my house from the outside, the glass would've been in the sink, on the kitchen countertop. But the window had shattered onto the ground below, which must mean someone wanted us to think the prowler got in through the window. Why? It had to be so the police wouldn't suspect they had let themselves in with a key.

Doc Nichols had a key to my back door so he could get in to take care of Hairy, but I had only given it to him that morning. On the night of the fire, only one other person besides myself had a key to my apartment.

"Mary George, if I don't get something to eat pretty soon, I'm going to be sick," Fronie said. "That looks like a right shady place up ahead there. Why don't you pull off and I'll fix us a plate of lunch?"

"We don't have time to stop," I said. "Just reach back there and grab something from the basket."

But Fronie grabbed her stomach instead and leaned forward with a horrible groan. "Oh, Lord, you've got to stop! I'm sick as a dog! Must be that candy bar I ate back there . . ." And she made the kind of noise you don't like to hear when you've just washed and vacuumed your car.

I pulled off onto a wide sandy turnaround and Fronie slid out and disappeared behind the large oaks that shaded the area. My hand hesitated over the button that locks the doors. I could leave her here and drive away. I could, and I wanted to. But what if I was wrong? The woman seemed genuinely ill. If something happened to her, I would be responsible.

My handbag with the Bible inside was jammed between my seat and the driver's side door within reassuring touch, and I felt inside to be sure the Good Book was there. Even though it had never left my side, it was comforting to feel the bulky shape, the worn old cover—and something else. Some kind of paper folded in half.

I'd almost forgotten the page from *Troublesome Creek Cooks* I had found on my seat earlier. Now I drew it out and looked at the recipe once more. I was right. Aunt Caroline had hurriedly circled the recipe for the coffee dessert, and below the directions and list of ingredients was the name of the person who had submitted it. Fronie Temple.

She had the door open before I could snap the lock and drive away. She also had a gun. A revolver. It could've been a toy, but it looked like a real one to me, and the barrel was pointed in my direction.

"Just pull on around behind those trees," Fronie directed. "Wouldn't want anybody seeing us from the road." And she stuck that ugly thing right in my face.

With the barrel nudging my ear, I backed and turned down a red dirt trail bordered by blackberry bushes and scrub pine. Overgrown now, probably it had once been used as a field road, and the car bucked and bumped over ruts and stones, limbs squeaked against the sides. Cautiously I crept around a sharp curve, then came to a sudden stop. A large pine had fallen across the road.

"Why are you stopping?" Fronie demanded.

I pointed to the obstacle in front of us. "I can't go any farther."

"Then give me the keys and get out."

From the half-open window came the fresh smell of pine, but the July heat was stifling, and the only thing that moved was the powdery copper dust settling around us. When would they find me here?

Something happened to me then. A cooling spring of calmness welled inside me, and I knew I didn't want to die. I jerked the keys from the ignition and tossed them out the window, tossed them into the rust-frosted tangle of weeds. I couldn't fight this crazy woman with a gun, but I could make things tough for the old witch.

And that's exactly what she looked like with her Halloween hair and her ridiculous striped hat. "Guess you'll have to hitchhike now," I said, and waited to meet my Maker.

But I guess my Maker wasn't receiving visitors because nothing happened. Tossing her hat onto the seat

194

behind her, Fronie opened her door and tramped around to mine. "Get out!" she said. "Get out and find them. You'll crawl around on your hands and knees until you do, Miss High and Mighty." And she wrenched open my door and prodded my shoulder with the gun. The gun gave Fronie power and she liked that. She could make me do what she wanted, but she couldn't control how I did it, or what I said. Fronie Temple needed me. For now.

"You killed Aunt Caroline," I said. And I knew it was true. She didn't deny it. "All along," I said, "you've been after this Bible. My Bible. Why? What possible use is it to you?"

Fronie leaned against the car and smiled. "I told you I had relatives in Hunters' Oak—*relative*, that is. Your long-lost great-uncle Benjamin was my husband's uncle too—my first husband, Fain. He and your father were first cousins. Fain died before I came here, before I married Braswell Temple, but he's closer kin to the old man than you are. As his widow, I'm entitled to inherit what would've come to him."

With one hand Fronie wiped the moisture from her brow, and with the other she waved the gun in my direction, all the time keeping distance between us. "Hurry up—look over there—in those weeds yonder!"

I dropped to my knees, but I wasn't looking for the keys, I was looking for a rock, a sharp stick, anything I could use as a weapon against her. If what she said was true, Fain Murphy must have descended from the third son, Ben's brother Horace. Fain was the cousin who died in Korea.

"Does Uncle Ben know about you?" I asked, pretending to search the grass.

"Of course he does. I was over there not too long ago,

195

took him a loaf of my apple-broccoli bread. Fain was his father's only surviving child, you know, and his uncle was fond of him in his way." She slapped at a mosquito. "I like to think he's fond of me as well. I'm sure he means to remember me in his will—after all, who else does he have to leave it to?"

Well, there was me, but in my present situation, I sort of hated to remind her.

All those years the family Bible had sat on the bookshelf in Aunt Caroline's living room and nobody paid a bit of attention to it. "Why now?" I asked. "Have you always known who I was?"

"Never even thought of it until I mentioned to Caroline once that my first husband came from Hunters' Oak and she said your people had lived there too. Since they had the same last name, I suggested maybe they were related. That's when Caroline told me about the Bible. 'We could look it up' she said. But we never did. That was twelve or thirteen years ago, soon after I came here.

"Besides, I got the notion the wonderful Miss Caroline would just as soon not have family connections with the likes of me!" Fronie sniffed. "Anyway, I forgot all about it, and so did she, I reckon, until that article came out in the paper about Ben."

The woman moved closer to stand over me, her footsteps sounded like a death rattle in the dry grass. "I don't think you're trying, Mary George, I really don't." She drew a wide circle with her foot. "Scrape up all the leaves here, pine needles too. They've got to be here somewhere. I'll wait." And she made herself comfortable in the shade of a hickory tree. I knew it was a hickory tree because I kept finding last year's squirrel-chewed nut shells. If I had a rubber band I could shoot them at her like David did to Goliath—only I'd probably miss. But when Fronie wasn't looking, I scooped a palmful of sandy soil into the pocket of my skirt.

"If your aunt hadn't become so suspicious, she'd be alive today," Fronie said, fanning herself with a small branch of leaves. "She showed me that Bible, don't you know, right after she came across it last spring. Forgot all about my Fain being kin too, and naturally I didn't mention it.

"But when I'd ask her about the Bible after that, she'd put me off, said she didn't know where it was." When Fronie Temple smiled she reminded me of a dog baring its teeth. She smiled now. "She knew very well where it was.

"She and that Delia—always thought they were so high muckety-muck, them and their I'll Try Society! Well, she's not so special now!"

Aunt Caroline had taught me we weren't supposed to hate, but I hated Fronie Temple. Hated her greed and her vanity and her selfishness—traits common to most of us to a certain degree, but Fronie Temple was just slapdab evil. "You didn't have to kill her," I said.

"Oh, but I did. I had to stop her, didn't I, before you saw where you belonged on the family tree? It should've stopped right there. You never would've known. The old man would die, I would inherit, and that would be that." Fronie stroked the grip of her revolver. "I really did care for your Aunt Caroline in spite of her being such a snob. She was good to help with my music, and don't think I'm not grateful. Why, it was me who got the music committee to commission Caroline's portrait."

"Kent Coffey. And he was to look for the Bible while

he painted, I suppose?" I added a rock to my pile of debris, but it was too small to do any good.

"Certainly not! Why, that was before I even knew Fain's uncle Ben was still alive." She seemed genuinely insulted. "Kent came to me as a tenant—such a good-looking young man, don't you think? But he was always short of money, and I'd seen some of his work, so I recommended him for the job. As far as I know, the portrait turned out just fine, although God knows what he did with it."

This woman either didn't know the difference between right and wrong, or she just didn't give a damn. I knew now Fronie had written the note "from Delia" I'd found on my door, and I'm sure she never called the barbecue place at all. It must have been Fronie watching from across the street when I left Delia's that night we found the key in the cookie jar. I wondered if she'd left a tape of herself singing so I'd think she never left home.

Through the trees I could see cars passing on the road behind her, but no one would think to look for me here. By now Delia and Sam would know something was wrong, but they'd never suspect Fronie Temple. My knees ached from squatting and I scratched a couple of ant bites on my leg. My mouth felt as dry as the dust in my pocket and sweat trickled slowly down my cheek, oozed between my breasts. I thought of the cool creek at Summerwood, rain splashing on sidewalks, a tall glass of ice water.

Fronie sipped from a Thermos of iced tea she'd taken from her hamper and glanced at her watch. "Keep looking, Mary George. We have plenty of daylight yet." She pointed to a patch of weeds behind me. "Why haven't you looked over there?"

I hadn't looked over there because that was where I threw the keys—or at least I thought it was. But the gun was persuasive, so I obliged, adding a little more dirt to my supply. I hoped she wouldn't notice the bulging pocket. Fronie had resumed her seat under the tree and I looked up to find her staring at me with an expression that made me almost as nervous as the gun. She rattled the ice in her cup and drained the contents.

"And how did you find Kent?" she asked.

"What do you mean, how did I find him?"

Fronie showed her teeth again. "I think you know what I mean." Gold gleamed from the crowns in her mouth. "I found him rather attractive," she said. "And I'm sure he felt the same way about me." She giggled girlishly. "A woman can sense these things."

"He set that fire, didn't he?" I wanted to throw up.

"Actually I did that," Fronie admitted. "Kent had some rather peculiar standards, but he did keep an eye on you for me. Actually, I think he rather enjoyed it, Mary George. You bewitched him, I'm afraid. Got to where I just couldn't trust him. Pity. The two of us would have been good for each other. Why, he might've lived rent free."

I thought of the radio announcement about the white Honda going off the side of the mountain and it made me sick. I don't know how she managed it, but I knew Fronie Temple was responsible, just as I knew she had used that woman's car to run down Bonita Moody. And poor Bonita hadn't the least idea who Fronie was.

And now it was my time.

"You've fooled around long enough!" Fronie Temple threw down her cup and stalked in circles about me. "I can see I'll have to look for those keys myself. You can either help me find them or stand there until I do. I'm

199

going to have to kill you anyway—it really doesn't matter when. Nobody's going to hear. Nobody's going to see."

I stood slowly, my heart melting into the red soil at my feet. I was so scared my teeth locked together. I couldn't yell if I wanted to. Was I really going to die? Had Augusta Goodnight saved me for this?

I remembered the angel sitting on Aunt Caroline's stairs in her little green suit and her frilly dot of a hat. How she'd jolted me back to reality with the sound of her no-nonsense voice. "I've had about enough of that," she'd said.

And so had I. This woman had a weapon, but I had one too. Little David used a stone to topple the giant. I would sting Fronie Temple where it hurt the most, and her weakness would bring her down.

# CHAPTER 24

MY BACK ACHED. I STRETCHED. AND OH, IT FELT SO good!

"Why are you smiling? What are you doing?" Fronie stepped away from me. "Be still! You stay right there."

This woman was stupid. Rotten and mean and stupid. This was going to be fun. I let go with the first of my ammunition. "It's too late, Fronie," I said. "A lot of people know about that Bible now. If anything happens to me, it won't do you any good, you won't even be able to inherit. Don't you think they might figure out who would benefit by my death?

"You know, I just don't believe you've been thinking. You are capable of thinking, aren't you?"

"What?" She lowered the gun, just a little.

"You brought poppyseed muffins to Aunt Caroline the day you made her fall, so she had to let you in. You brought them on that pink-flowered plate, and when I ate one, it was stale. It was stale because they'd been there since *before* she died. But you didn't think about that."

"I really can't see that it matters." She held the gun stiffly in front of her. "Don't you get any closer now."

Keeping an eye on her, I inched slowly backward. I knew my aunt, and no matter how suspicious she was of Fronie Temple, Aunt Caroline would have accepted the muffins graciously. Courtesy was ingrained in her, but it betrayed her in the end.

"You followed her into the kitchen with them, all the time pretending to be her friend," I said. "But she knew something was wrong. I guess she just didn't realize how far you'd go."

"How do you know? You'd never be able to prove it!" Fronie took a step closer. "Not that you'll be around that long."

The two of them must have spent some time in the kitchen in order for Aunt Caroline to quickly circle Fronie's recipe in *Troublesome Creek Cooks*. The cookbook stayed in constant use, and was probably already open on her counter.

"In that case, you might as well tell me," I said. "You forced her into the attic, didn't you? But the Bible wasn't there."

Fronie Temple didn't answer, but her expression told me I was right. My heart, filled with fury and pain, wanted me to throw myself on her then and there, beat her into the ground. But my head told me to wait. Fronie had a gun. I didn't. Emotions would have to take a backseat. For now.

Somehow, while in the attic, Aunt Caroline had managed to slip the key to the post office box into the cookie jar. I think she had intended to mail it to me, probably that very day, and either had it in her pocket, or distracted Fronie long enough to put it there while they were in the kitchen. I didn't want to know how she died—whether she fell or was pushed, but I suspected the latter.

"What's done is done," Fronie Temple said. "Words aren't going to change it. You're just talking to hear yourself talk, but it's not going to work. I'm not listening to a word you're saying."

*Okay, Mary George*, I thought, *time for phase two.* "I'm *saying I* don't think you're very bright. Except for the clothes you wear—they're a little *too* bright, don't you think? Tacky, in fact. Tight too. You're not a size ten anymore, are you? And you're certainly no beauty queen. Poor Kent! No wonder he was in a hurry to get away. Get real! Do you really think he cared anything about you?" My smile grew broader. Each barb went in a little deeper. Each flinch brought me pleasure. I hoped my sweet aunt Caroline, wherever she was, would forgive me. And somehow, I knew she would.

Fronie's lip trembled. "You shut up! I'll be glad to be rid of the both of you—you and that big, ugly dog. I wish he'd run in front of a truck when I ran him off before."

"That was you following me, wasn't it? The day I went to Hughes, to Summerwood. You were driving that woman's car."

"Oh, that. I thought you were on the way to your uncle's in Hunters' Oak. Had to find some way to stop you." She shrugged. "Well, you got by me that time."

"What were you going to do, run me off the road?"

As soon as I said it, I knew it was true. I remembered an unusually narrow and dangerous stretch between Hughes and High Point. Thank goodness we had been able to give her the slip. "It really didn't take a lot to outwit you, Fronie," I said softly.

She looked like she'd been slapped. "Why are you saying these things to me?"

My hand closed around the dirt in my pocket, I moved a step closer. "Because they're true. And that's not all. You'd think you could at least follow a recipe, but your cooking stinks too. Isn't fit to eat. Remember those squash 'wads' on the Fourth of July? Kent and I buried them in the park—without honors."

Ohmygosh! She lifted the gun, but her hand trembled, and her face was about the same color as her lipstick. Fronie Temple had probably shoved Aunt Caroline down the stairs, run down Bonita Moody in the dark of night, and no telling what she'd done to Kent Coffey, but having to shoot somebody face to face was playing on her nerves. A tremor went through her.

"Actually, I think your singing's the worst," I said. "A joke. Everybody's laughing. Half the congregation wears earplugs." I was getting high on this. Why hadn't I thought of this earlier?

"Stop! That's not true!" When Fronie Temple screamed, I let fly a fistful of dirt as close to her eyes as I could get and dived for her knees.

The gun flew somewhere in the bushes, and Fronie doubled over like a big bag of laundry and landed on her hands and knees in the dirt. "You can't talk to me like that! I'll show you!" Crying, she started crawling toward a tangle of honeysuckle on the fallen log and I saw the ugly gleam of metal beneath the leaves.

"Oh, no, you don't!" I sprang over her back like a

child playing leapfrog and stomped hard on her outstretched fingers just as she reached for the gun.

This time I think Fronie Temple actually hit high F— and she'd been trying for years, but she didn't seem pleased about it. When the screaming and jumping around subsided, she saw that I held the gun, and I'll swear if her attitude didn't do a complete turnaround.

"I don't know what came over me, Mary George," she said with a sickly little smile. "It must be my medication. Heart palpitations, don't you know? Nerves, the doctor says. Pure stress. I just can't imagine what made me do that."

"Ask me if I care," I said, and got a firmer grip on the revolver. I can't stand guns, don't even like to touch them, but I couldn't take a chance on this crazy woman getting her hands on it again. But what was I going to do with her? And where on earth were the keys to my car?

Then a gleam caught my eye, and there they were in plain sight just a few feet away in a spot where I was sure I'd looked earlier. And when I picked them up, I knew Augusta was there. Well, it was about time.

"Fronie, old girl," I said, "I'm afraid I'm going to have to leave you here for a while. Why don't you make yourself comfortable under that nice tree, and I imagine somebody will be along to see to you in a little while." I squinted at the sun. "As you said, there's plenty of daylight left."

"Where are you going? What are you going to do? You're not going to leave me here in the middle of nowhere?"

"Oh, but I am. Can't very well drive and keep an eye on you, can I? I wouldn't touch that door handle, Fronie. That's right, get away from the car—way away.

204

Somebody should be here shortly."

"But I won't try anything . . . really. You don't have to worry about me . . . I wouldn't hurt you, Mary George. I wouldn't hurt anybody . . ."

I could still hear her pleading as I backed the car to turn around. I hoped she would be there by the time the police came.

"Quick thinking, Mary George Murphy! I'd say you handled that situation very well." Suddenly Augusta was beside me beaming.

"And no thanks to you. Those car keys were right under her nose. If Fronie had seen them, I'd have been a goner."

"Ah, but she wasn't going to see them," my angel said.

"Damn it, Augusta, how do you know? You weren't even there."

Augusta ran her fingers through her long, gingery hair and let it flow behind her. "Oh, I do wish you'd watch your language. Not only was I there, she said, "but I was standing on them."

"Well, well," Uncle Ben said, "I've always wanted to identify myself with that droll adventurer, Mark Twain, and I'm delighted to see we actually have something in common."

"And how is that?" Sam asked.

"The reports of my death—impending death, in my case—are greatly exaggerated."

My face turned hot, and if the table hadn't had a glass top, I might have crawled under it, but my uncle's uncluttered sunroom offered no such place to hide.

Our dinner together had been postponed after my

205

unfortunate confrontation with phony Fronie, and now, a couple of weeks later, Delia, Sam, and I were guests for a nutritious meal of pasta, and vegetables, fruit, and a delicious whole grain bread served warm with honey.

Uncle Ben himself, refreshed after a short nap following his daily three-mile swim, looked firm, fit, and not much over fifty—although he admitted to seventy, and was probably closer to eighty.

He seemed a happy man sitting there in his comfortable highbacked wicker chair with a cross-eyed Siamese in his lap and a brandy in his hand. "I've enjoyed good health, good friends, and a good, long life," he told us, stroking the cat's cream-and-brown back. "But now I'm getting my affairs in order."

And from the looks exchanged between my uncle and his attractive, middle-aged secretary, Ava, that wasn't all he was getting, I thought. No doubt about it, Uncle Ben was a happy man.

And a shrewd one. He had seen through Fronie Temple at once. "A coarse, yeller-haired baggage! That's what she was when poor, gullible Fain married her, and that's what she is today. Why, the silly woman actually tried to flirt with me. I can't imagine why she'd think I'd leave her one cent." My uncle pondered his brandy. "No class. Absolutely no class at all."

"No conscience either, apparently," Delia said. "They found sleeping pills dissolved in the Thermos of coffee in that fellow's car—the one who went off the mountain. He must've fallen asleep."

Kent Coffey had suffered severe injuries and it would be a good long time before he'd be able to live normally. Fortunately he had managed to crawl away from the wreckage before his car fell to the bottom of the deep ravine.

In a way, I guess Kent was lucky. And so was I. Not only had Sam and I found each other, but Delia was going to take over the business end of Camp Summerwood, and with Cindy coming back as cook, we had a good start on our staff.

I say "our staff" even though I'm not on it, not officially anyway, unless you count weekend volunteers. But I start back to school part-time this fall, and if all goes well, I should be able to get my degree in a couple of years. And Uncle Ben—bless his big old fat checkbook—insists on paying my tuition, although I doubt I'll inherit a cent. After all, it looks like he's planning to hang on awhile longer, at least I hope he will. But Sam and I have persuaded him to set up an endowment for the camp. The new main hall will be named for him, of course, and with continued support and a challenging faculty, such as Sam (and eventually me), Summerwood should soon be back on its feet.

Now the ceiling fan whirred as I sipped ice water with a wedge of lime. All afternoon I had kept an eye out for "Igor," listened for the heavy shuffle of his feet, but he had yet to put in an appearance. Maybe it was his day off.

My great-uncle Ben set aside his snifter, folded his hands, and looked at me. "If your friend Delia hadn't called to see if I'd heard from you when everything came to a boil the other day, I wouldn't have known what was going on."

Sam laughed. "Then I guess you didn't catch the five o'clock news. Delia and I were out scouting the countryside for Mary G. when they announced over the radio about Fronie and the tomato truck."

The image was so comical it made me forget my brief efforts to be dignified, and I giggled, picturing my former landlady rolling around in a load of produce.

It seems the driver of the truck had stopped to relieve himself near the spot where I left Fronie and she took the opportunity to hitch a ride in back while he wasn't looking.

Fortunately, the police caught up with them a few miles down the road, but not before the troopers' car got "bombed" with exploding red fruit.

"I knew something was wrong," Sam told him, "when Mary G. didn't show up for barbecue. She might stand me up, but she'd never turn down a good batch of Brunswick stew, so I gave Delia a call and she was just about frantic."

"Fronie had phoned earlier pretending to be someone calling from the vet's," Delia said. "Told me Mary George asked her to say she'd be leaving an hour later than we planned. Of course when I went to meet her she was already gone, and Doc Nichols said nobody had called from there."

Uncle Ben shook his head. "Fronie won't be calling anybody for a long time now, except maybe her lawyer!"

He narrowed his eyes and frowned at me. "Mary George Murphy, why *do* you keep twisting about in that chair? Would you like a pillow, or do you need to be excused?"

"Sorry. I was kind of hoping to meet your butler Igor—I mean, what's his name? Milford . . . What? What's so funny?"

My uncle laughed until tears trickled down his well-preserved old cheeks. "There is no Milford," he said when he finally stopped for breath.

"No Milford? Then who answered the phone when I called? Said you couldn't be disturbed. That was you . . . *you*! It was you, wasn't it?"

My uncle winked at me and smiled. "Somebody has to screen my calls. Besides, when you get to be my age, you have to liven things up once in a while.

"Now, don't look at me like that, my dear. Just because I concocted an imaginary butler doesn't necessarily mean I'm crazy. We all need a little fantasy now and then."

"I won't argue with that," I said.

But had Augusta Goodnight been a fantasy? Someone I invented out of my own desperation? No one had seen her but me, and after Fronie's tomato chase and subsequent incarceration, she had appeared for shorter durations. And there was a wistful kind of joy about her. She reminded me of the way Aunt Caroline looked the night I graduated from Troublesome Creek High. I knew she was trying to tell me good-bye.

The smell of coffee greeted me when I got home from my uncle's that night. Strong coffee. And there Augusta sat in the kitchen with the half-empty pot at her elbow. When she saw me, she smiled and raised her cup. "To you, Mary George Murphy. Congratulations."

"You're leaving me," I said. "Why?"

"You can take care of yourself. And very well, I might add. My job here is done." And she quickly rose and kissed me, brushed my cheek with her strawberry-scented lips. I heard a soft sort of flutter and my eyes got swimmy hot. "I'll miss you, Augusta," I whispered.

"Don't cry, now," she said. And I didn't. I closed my eyes for a minute, and when I opened them she was gone. But there's a sweet, brave place inside me that wasn't there before.

Dear Reader:

I hope you enjoyed reading this Large Print mystery. If you are interested in reading other Beeler Large Print Mystery titles or any other Beeler Large Print titles, ask your librarian or write to me at

Thomas T. Beeler, *Publisher*
Post Office Box 659
Hampton Falls, New Hampshire 03844

You can also call me at 1-800-251-8726 and I will send you my latest catalogue.

Audrey Lesko chooses the titles I publish in Large Print. Our aim is to provide good books by outstanding authors—books we both enjoyed reading and liked well enough to want to share. We warmly welcome any suggestions for new titles and authors.

Sincerely,